W9-AHW-763

#3

DATE DUE

SEP 2 4 2008			
DEC 0 3 2008			
12-17-08			
AUG 1 0 2009			
SEP 0 5 2009 AL			

LANEY'S KISS

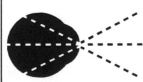

This Large Print Book carries the
Seal of Approval of N.A.V.H.

KANSAS HOME, BOOK 3

LANEY'S KISS

A HEART ADRIFT FINDS A PLACE TO DWELL IN THIS ROMANTIC STORY

TRACEY V. BATEMAN

THORNDIKE PRESS
A part of Gale, Cengage Learning

GALE
CENGAGE Learning

Detroit • New York • San Francisco • New Haven, Conn • Waterville, Maine • London

GALE
CENGAGE Learning™

LIBRARY OF CONGRESS CATALOGING-IN-PUBLICATION DATA

Bateman, Tracey Victoria.
    Laney's kiss : a heart adrift finds a place to dwell in this
romantic story / by Tracey V. Bateman.
        p. cm. — (Kansas home ; bk. 3) (Thorndike Press large print
Christian romance)
    ISBN-13: 978-1-4104-0857-0 (alk. paper)
    ISBN-10: 1-4104-0857-4 (alk. paper)
    1. Large type books. I. Title.
PS3602.A854L36 2008
813'.6—dc22   2008018773

Published in 2008 by arrangement with Barbour Publishing, Inc.

Printed in the United States of America
1 2 3 4 5 6 7 12 11 10 09 08

For my sister, Sandy.
Your strength of character amazes me.
Your ability to consistently achieve your
goals inspires me.
Your humanness humbles me.
In all of your strengths and weaknesses
—

to God be the glory for making you who
you are.
All my love,
T

PROLOGUE

"I cain't believe Pa just up and gave us away," Laney said hotly.

The relief Tarah had expected from the children was replaced by the reality of indignation and hurt, emotions she had never expected from them.

"He ain't givin' us away, Laney," Ben said with a scowl.

"Do ya think I'm dumb? I got ears. Pa said we was Tarah's now. If that ain't givin' a person away, I don't rightly know what is."

"Pa sold us," he said curtly.

"Yer crazy," Laney retorted.

"Why do ya think Anthony and Tarah's walkin'? Pa got ol' Dodger, and I seen Tarah give 'im some cash money, too."

Laney's mouth dropped open, and she regarded Tarah and Anthony with disbelief. "You mean, you bought me and Ben like we was slaves?"

7

"No, sweetie," Tarah said. "We did what we had to do so you don't have to go back to your pa."

"Ya said we was like family," Laney said bitterly. "But we ain't. We're just slaves, bought and paid fer."

Tarah grabbed the reins and halted Abby. She laid her palm on Laney's jean-clad knee and met her accusing glare.

"You know Cassidy isn't my blood ma, right? And Emily isn't my blood sister?"

Laney nodded.

"But I love them as dearly as if they were blood kin. And Hope and Will are no less my brother and sister than Luke and Sam and Jack and Emily," she said, giving Laney a gentle smile. "It doesn't matter how you become a family. All that matters is that you love one another."

To Tarah's relief, Laney's face softened reflectively.

"And you really can keep us always?"

"Always."

Laney inclined her head. "Then I reckon we oughtta be gettin' home b'fore yer ma starts worryin'."

CHAPTER 1

A man's heart deviseth his way:
but the LORD directeth his steps.

PROVERBS 16:9

1879, Kansas

Laney Jenkins glared at the man sitting tall astride a gelding as red as its master's hair. "One more word, and I'm going to flatten you, Luke St. John."

She could admit she was a little dusty from the trail, and who wouldn't need a bath to wash away the smell and grime after two weeks of herding cattle? But that didn't give Luke any right to insult her.

A shrug lifted his well-muscled shoulders. "I stand by what I said. You're as dirty as you were the first time I laid eyes on you." Luke's lazy grin infuriated Laney all the more. "I remember you walked into the school looking and smelling like you'd just had a tumble with a herd of pigs."

9

Laney's ire rose, and she clutched the leather reins, fighting for control over her raging emotions. She felt grimy from driving the cattle to Abilene, tired from her turn at keeping watch last night, and her behind ached from day after day of sitting on the hard seat of the supply wagon.

She hated the trip more each time she made it. Going along with Papa Dell and the ranch hands had started out as an adventure, but she would have stopped after the first drive if not for Luke suggesting she was too much of a tenderfoot to endure the hardship. Now, enduring the hardship was a matter of principle.

But she'd made her point once again, and home was only a few miles away. She longed for a leisurely hot bath, a home-cooked meal, and a good night's sleep in her own bed. She certainly didn't need Luke's insults. Nor would she stand for them.

"Luke," she said slowly, warning thick in her voice. "I mean it. You hush up, or I'm going to knock you off that horse and give you a sound thrashing."

"I doubt you could," he challenged, his grin firmly planted on his freckled face. "Besides, when are you going to start acting like a girl? Or do you even know how?"

"I — you —" she sputtered. Oh, why

10

could she never come up with a good retort to put him in his place?

"Close your mouth before you swallow a bug," Luke baited.

"That's it!" Laney shot from the wagon seat, propelled her body toward Luke, and knocked him from his horse. His startled cry gave Laney more than a little satisfaction as they landed together on the rain-deprived earth. Ignoring the pain in her left leg, she held on to his shoulders and rolled, waiting for an opportunity to whale the daylights out of him. In a flash, he overpowered her. He straddled her, pinning her hands to the ground with his palms.

"Stop it," he growled, his green eyes flashing mere inches above hers. "You know I can't hit you back."

"You couldn't get close enough to hit me, Luke St. John!" She glared up at him.

The corners of his lips twitched at her ridiculous statement. Something akin to a growl gargled in her throat, and she kicked fruitlessly against the ground beneath her heels. She gave a violent twist, trying to free herself.

"Cut it out." Luke pressed harder on her hands, his face screwed up in disgust. "I don't know what's got into you lately. You can't even take a little teasing anymore."

"Maybe I'm just sick of you," she spat. "Ever think of that?" Being this near to Luke, feeling his warm breath on her face, was too achingly close for comfort. If he didn't let her up soon, she'd most likely do something stupid like throw her arms around him and declare her love right then and there.

"I'll let you up if you promise to stop acting so ignorant and get back in the wagon."

"Sounds like a good idea." A shadow fell across them, accompanying the stern voice. Laney glanced up to find Luke's tall, lean pa astride his mount. Brows furrowed, he glared down at his son. "Get off of her. I didn't raise you to manhandle women."

Luke's face reddened, making his freckles pop out even farther. He stood and reached down for Laney.

Laney grasped his hand and felt herself being hauled upright. The thick tension passing between father and son felt almost tangible, and guilt pricked her.

"It was my fault, Papa Dell. I — I took offense to something Luke said."

Dell glanced sternly at Luke. "What have I told you about the way you speak to Laney? I've half a mind to let her give you a sound whipping."

Luke slapped his Stetson hard against his

thigh. Laney cringed, knowing his action was more from frustration than the need to dust off his hat. Now he'd be madder than ever. Mad at her.

With his eyes as cold as emeralds, Luke pressed his hat against his chest and gave her an exaggerated bow. "I apologize from the bottom of my heart, fair Laney. I should never have suggested you aren't the epitome of ladyhood."

Laney wasn't sure *ladyhood* was even a word, but the implication hit her full in the stomach. Heat rushed to her cheeks. She clenched her fists and swept a sideways glance at Papa Dell. No. She'd better not tear into Luke right now, or she'd get the same scolding he was getting.

"We can do without the sarcasm," Papa Dell drawled. "Now mount up, and let's get home."

"Yes, Pa," Luke mumbled.

With a satisfied nod, Papa Dell turned his horse and rode after the three ranch hands who appeared as mere dots on the horizon. Luke's gaze followed his pa's retreating form. Laney could see the struggle in his expression, and her heart went out to him, sifting the anger from her like a sieve. The two men often disagreed about the ranch. Luke complained that his pa was too set in

13

his ways, and the older man always said there was no reason to change what had worked well for over twenty years. No one could deny that the St. John ranch prospered more than any ranch in the area, but Laney had to wonder why his pa couldn't at least consider some of Luke's ideas.

Clearing her throat, she reached out tentatively, then stopped short of touching Luke's arm as he turned to her, eyes blazing.

"Get in the wagon, and let's get out of here."

That was the last time she'd try apologizing to him! "Well, you don't have to be such an ol' bear about it. It's not my fault your pa rode back to check on us and caught you pinning me to the ground."

"Which," Luke said through gritted teeth, "I wouldn't have been doing if you hadn't knocked me off my horse in the first place."

Hands on her hips, Laney stamped her foot and glared back at him. "You shouldn't have suggested I don't act like a girl."

"Suggested? I'm saying plain as day you don't act like a woman. Just look at you." Reaching forward, he flicked her Stetson from her head.

"Hey!" Snatching at the air, Laney made a futile attempt to catch the hat before it landed on the ground. Leaving it, she glowered. "Wearing britches and a hat don't make me no less a woman than a person in ruffles and petticoats."

"I didn't say you're less of a woman. I said you don't act like the rest of them." He gave her a pointed look. "And you don't."

Narrowing her gaze, Laney sized him up. She cocked her head to the side. "What do you know about women anyway?"

Deep creases etched his brow. "Just forget about it, okay?"

"No," she challenged. "I want to know. Just how do you think a woman is supposed to act?" The air between them grew still as she waited. What sort of woman was Luke looking for? Could she ever measure up?

He hesitated a moment, regarding her frankly. "You know, all soft and . . . womanly. I don't know, Laney. Just let it be."

"Womanly?" Dejectedly Laney glanced down at her faded britches and ripped shirt. Soft and womanly pretty much excluded her from the list of possible candidates for Luke's affection.

He looked pensively toward the orange horizon, where the sun was making a final bow before disappearing into the night sky. A sense of foreboding coursed through Laney at the faraway look in his eyes.

"What do you mean by 'womanly'?"

He shifted his gaze back to her, searching. Laney's heart pounded in her ears at his uncharacteristically intense manner. He spoke slowly, thoughtfully. "A man wants a woman he can take into his arms and feel like she needs him to protect her." Laney stiffened as a hint of the old teasing creased the corners of his eyes. "In all the years I've known you, you've never once even let me lead a dance."

Laney smarted under his criticism and was about to retort when he strode forward and retrieved her hat from the ground. He towered over her tiny frame. The angry words fled her mind as he placed the Stetson gently atop her head and looked down into her eyes. "You're a pretty girl, Laney."

Laney's hopes soared at his words and then sank as he continued. "But pretty isn't all a man wants." He smiled an almost bitter smile. "You don't need anyone to take care of you. You can outride, outshoot, and outtrack most of the men living in and around Harper, and everyone knows it. A fellow doesn't want a wife who's more of a man than he is." He laughed. "You'd probably expect your husband to scrub the floors and cook the food you shoot."

His laughter was all the humiliation Laney

could take. There was only one way to prove to him she was as much of a woman as any of the frilly, eye-batting, teeth-flashing ninnies of Harper out to trap him into matrimony.

With a determined lift of her chin, she took a step closer until she stood mere inches from him.

"What are you doing?" Suspicion thickened his tone, and he moved back.

Silently she took another step forward without breaking his startled gaze. Then before she could change her mind or he could get away, she inched her arms upward until they clasped behind his neck.

"What do you think you're —"

Without a word, Laney rose up on her toes and kissed him full on the lips. He stood motionless for only an instant, then his arms encircled her waist, pressing her closer. Laney's senses reeled as her plan backfired and Luke took control. His mouth moved over hers until she clung to him. When he gently released her, they stood for a moment, gazes locked, chests heaving.

"Do you want to tell me what that was all about?" Luke asked, visibly shaken, but scowling as if he hadn't responded to the kiss.

Laney stepped back.

"Well?" he asked.

"D–don't ever say I'm not a woman again!"

Giving him no chance to respond, she spun around on the heel of her boot and stomped to Luke's horse, Rusty. She mounted the gelding.

"What do you think you're doing?"

"I'm sick of that wagon." She glared down at him, daring him to try to stop her. "You take it to the ranch. I'm going straight home."

"Okay, fine. I'll be over tomorrow to pick up my horse."

"Fine." Needing to distance herself from him as quickly as possible, Laney nudged the horse into a gallop and left Luke standing beside the wagon.

The memory of Luke's lips on hers taunted Laney as she headed for Harper. She squirmed under the humiliation. How could she have been so stupid? Now Luke would know she cared for him. Things would never be the same again.

A cloud of dust rose up around Laney as she sped away. Luke stared after her, shaking his head. *She ought to have more sense than to ride Rusty so hard after weeks on the trail.*

He climbed onto the wagon seat and flapped the reins. What had crazy little Laney been thinking, kissing him like that? She couldn't even let a man make the first move. Not that he ever would have. He'd never thought of Laney romantically. But he had to admit, their kiss was something. Even now, the memory of her soft, full lips beneath his stirred him.

With a frustrated grunt, Luke tried to remove the image of her wide, doelike eyes staring up at him in wonder after he released her. It wasn't like he'd never kissed a girl before. He'd stolen plenty of kisses behind the schoolhouse and on buggy rides, but none had affected him like this one.

Whatever possessed him to draw her into his arms and respond to her kiss the way he had? Laney, of all people! She'd grown up in his older sister, Tarah's, home. Luke and Laney had played together, fished together, hunted together, and for the past two years worked the ranch together. But mostly they fought. Luke grinned in spite of his confusion. Laney could get riled up quicker than an ol' tomcat stuck in a tree, and he knew just how to get her spittin' mad. To her credit, she never held a grudge. Once she said her piece, that was that and she was ready to be friends again.

His friend, his buddy, his pal . . . or was their kiss an indication there was more than friendship between them?

Luke chided himself for the idiotic thought worming its way into his mind. He shook his head. How could there be anything romantic between them? That was about the dumbest thing he'd ever thought of. And it was her fault. If she hadn't been so fired up to prove she was a woman — and she'd pretty well made her point — he wouldn't be so addlepated about everything.

He stared into the dusky sky. Things would never be the same between them again. She'd expect him to court her now. And she'd be within her rights to expect it after the way he'd kissed her.

Luke slapped at his thigh. He'd made a big mess of things by not throwing her away from him and giving her a good chewing out for even trying to kiss him. If only it hadn't seemed so right. . . .

"What do you mean, you aren't going to the dance tonight?"

Seated on the edge of her bed, Laney forced herself to meet Tarah Greene's gaze head-on. "Exactly what I said. I'm staying home."

"Now you listen to me, Laney Jenkins.

You've been moping around this house for two weeks — always making excuses not to go to the ranch or even to church. Are you going to tell me what happened on that trail, or am I going to have to go ask Pa?"

Laney knew better than to try to skirt around the issue any longer. When Tarah tossed her head of coal-black hair, she meant business.

Laney threw herself across her bed, landing on her stomach, chin planted firmly in her palm. "I kissed Luke," she admitted flatly, wishing for all she was worth the episode had been only another of her delicious dreams instead of a wretched bit of reality.

After a moment of silence, Laney turned her head to see if Tarah was still in the room. Tarah grinned as Laney's gaze found hers. "Are you telling me you and Luke are courting now?"

"No. He was teasing me, as usual, about not acting like a girl, and I just . . . up and kissed him." Laney emitted a low groan. "He makes me so mad, Tarah. Always insinuating I'm somewhere between a male and female just because I like to wear britches and boots." Laney gave a frustrated wave of her hand. "So what did I do? I had to go and show him I'm all woman."

Tarah lowered herself carefully to the bed beside Laney. "Believe me," she said, her lips twitching, "as Luke's sister and former schoolteacher, I know how infuriating he can be. The thing that surprises me is your reaction to it after all these years. I would have expected you to ignore him or punch him . . . but a kiss? Where did that come from?"

"From me, unfortunately." Laney heaved a sigh as she stared morosely at the ceiling. "Now he'll probably think I want him to court me like some weak-kneed sissy-girl with a lacy parasol."

"You know, Laney, there's no shame in being a woman. And looking like one," Tarah said with a pointed glance at Laney's faded britches. "And there's nothing wrong with wanting a man to court you."

She shrugged. "It's okay for other women — just not for me, that's all. It's not like I don't wear skirts when I go to town or for church on Sunday. But I have to wear britches on the ranch. How can I herd cattle in a dress? And if Luke wants the kind of woman who faints and flutters, then I wasted a perfectly good kiss on a big, dumb . . . dumb . . . !" She hated it when she couldn't think of just the right insult, even if he wasn't in the room to hear it.

"Honestly, Laney. Don't fret about it." Tarah stood as gracefully as her protruding stomach would allow and planted her hands on her hips, rounded from bearing three babies in the past eight years. "Don't wear a dress on the ranch and at home if you'd rather not — you know, no one in the family cares about that. And don't waste any more kisses on Luke — although it served him right that you gave him one in the first place. But you *have* to come to the dance. Half the women there will be wearing gowns you made. You never know how many orders you might get for more, once word gets out that you made the prettiest dresses at the dance."

The thought was tempting. Laney's mind floated to her growing nest egg. If she could sell a few more dresses, she'd have enough to put a down payment on the old soddy Mr. Garner was willing to sell to her along with five acres now with an option to buy more.

As if reading her mind, Tarah sighed heavily. "I hate the thought of you moving out. You should stay with us until you marry. Then you and your husband would have a fine start with the money you've socked away."

Laney's eyes widened. "Give my money to

23

a man? Are you crazy, Tarah? Pa took everything we had and drank it away. I'm going to make sure I have everything I need, and I'll never let a man boss me. No siree. That might be okay for some women, but not me — ever! When I marry, I'll make sure my property is protected so he can't take it and squander it all away. My young'uns will be taken care of."

Tarah gave her a pitying smile — one that carried a secret Laney felt she would never be privy to. "Laney, honey," Tarah said, "when you find a man who really loves you, he won't want to boss you around. You'll be partners."

Laney snorted.

"It's true." Tarah's smile widened, and she sent Laney a wink. "And you know what else?"

"What?" Laney asked, narrowing her gaze in suspicion.

"You'll gladly give him all the money you have, because you'll be able to trust him to use it wisely, and if he is a smart man — which I have no doubt he will be — he'll want all the input from you he can get about how to spend it."

Laney stood, inclining her head in a jerky nod. "I won't marry a dumb man. That's for sure. Still, I reckon I'll do it my way just in case he takes to drinking. That makes a man stupid real fast."

Tarah chuckled and hugged Laney tightly. "Oh, Laney. God has such a wonderful plan for your life. I only hope you're not too stubborn to let Him unfold it for you."

"God gave me a good head on my shoulders and two sturdy hands. I reckon He expects me to do the rest. And, Tarah, I fully intend to make sure I can take care of myself."

Laney squirmed under that pity-smile again.

"Then come out to the Moodys' farm for the dance. I could use your help with the kids."

Laney gave a short laugh. The whole town loved Reverend Greene, Tarah, and their three children. Once she walked through the barn doors, Tarah wouldn't see those children again until they were ready to leave.

Caught in her manipulation, Tarah gave her a sheepish grin and shrugged. "Okay, maybe I won't need help with the children, but you still have to go. We won't have nearly as much fun without you. Now come on. I took your blue skirt off the line today. I noticed it's getting a bit thin. You may want to take time out to sew another one before it's too threadbare to do any good.

Anyway, the tub's filled and waiting for you in the kitchen."

Unable to withstand Tarah's pleading eyes, Laney relented. "All right. But only because I might get some business out of it."

"Wonderful!" Tarah said, her violet eyes sparkling. "I'll leave you to get ready for your bath, then."

Laney watched the door close behind Tarah. Her stomach jumped at the thought of seeing Luke for the first time since their kiss. Would he act any differently? Would he ask her to dance like old times? She'd be careful to let him lead this time. Following wasn't easy for her, but she could do anything she set her mind to. Especially if it meant proving to Luke she was a woman.

Fleetingly her mind drifted to the blue silk gown in her wardrobe. The fashionable bustle was sure to make Luke take notice. As far as Laney knew, no one else would be wearing a bustle this evening. The woman who had commissioned the gown had gained at least fifteen pounds between the time she had ordered the dress and waited her turn for Laney to sew it. There wasn't enough material to make it fit, so Laney had to take a loss on the sale.

She walked to the wardrobe, opened it,

and fingered the delicate material. The loss of money might be worth the look in Luke's eyes when he saw her wearing this.

"Laney?" Tarah's voice drifted through the door.

Laney jumped and snatched her hand away as though she were a thief caught stealing priceless jewels. "What?" she snapped.

"If you don't take your bath right now, we'll be late for the dance."

"You all go on ahead of me. I'll get ready and follow on Colby."

"Are you sure, Laney? We can wait if you'll hurry."

"I'd rather ride."

Laney felt Tarah's hesitation.

"Honest, Tarah. You go on. The preacher's family can't be late. I'll be along soon. I promise."

"All right. We'll see you there."

Laney smiled at the relief in Tarah's tone. Laney always kept her promises. Tarah knew that and trusted her. The knowledge warmed Laney.

Laney Jenkins didn't lie, she didn't cheat, and she never, ever went back on her word no matter how much it cost her. She grabbed her simple muslin skirt and fresh blue gingham shirt from the wardrobe, then

27

slammed the wardrobe shut. Most of all she never, ever resorted to frills to win a man's attention. Luke would have to take her as she was, or he could forget it!

Dejectedly Laney studied her reflection in the vanity mirror. Luke had already told her what kind of woman he wanted, and she didn't come close to fitting his ideal. She jerked her chin. Oh well. Let him marry some snippy, drippy, fainting ninny. Laney Jenkins would be just fine on her own. Everything was going according to plan. If her dresses kept selling, she would soon have the down payment on her own land. She'd be self-reliant, and the Jenkins name would be brought to honor instead of the shame her pa had made of it.

Who needed Luke St. John, anyway?

CHAPTER 2

Laney's head pounded to the beat of "Camptown Races," and her toes suffered under the punishment of Clyde Hampton's shiny new boots.

She cast another hopeful glance toward the double doors of Mr. Moody's barn — which had been transformed for the harvest dance, as it was every year. The dance had been well under way for the past forty-five minutes, and still no Luke. Not that Laney cared if he missed the harvest dance. Why should she?

"Ow." Laney turned her gaze from the door and glared up at her dancing partner as pain shot through her big toe and up to her ankle. "Clyde, where'd you learn to dance, anyway?"

"I'm sorry, Miss Laney." The middle-aged sheep rancher's face turned as red as the handkerchief tied around his long, skinny neck. "Don't know what's got into me tonight. Seems I got two left feet."

"Oh, Clyde." Laney gave him an apologetic smile, suddenly feeling guilty for her churlish manner. "You're not that bad."

His face brightened. "Mighty kind of ya to say so, Miss Laney."

"May I cut in, Clyde?"

Laney's palms dampened at the sound of Luke's voice.

"Be my guest."

All the feelings of compassion she had previously felt for the bad dancer fled at the relief in Clyde's tone and the way he practically pushed her into Luke's arms.

"Clumsy oaf," she muttered as the rancher hurried from the dance floor. "I won't be able to wear my boots for a week."

Luke laughed and pulled her into the circle of his arms. "It's your own fault if your toes are bruised. You should have let him lead."

Laney huffed and stepped to her left, then stopped short as Luke stepped to her right. He laughed again. "See what I mean? Now concentrate real hard and try to follow."

"I wouldn't follow you if you were the last man on earth with two good legs, Luke St. John!" Laney squirmed, trying to free herself from his embrace.

"I'm probably the last man on earth even

willing to dance with the likes of you, Laney Jenkins," he retorted, releasing her.

Fury washed over her. "I can get any man here to dance with me, and they'd be proud to do it!"

"Simmer down. People are staring."

Laney glanced quickly around the room, observing the raised brows from a group of gray-haired matrons chatting in the corner and Papa Dell's disapproving frown from the other side of the room, where he stood talking with Anthony. She drew in a long, calming breath. Luke had the uncanny ability to get her riled enough to make a complete fool of herself, but this time she would not allow him to bait her.

With a step forward, she placed her hand on his shoulder and waited for him to take the other. "Lead," she commanded through gritted teeth.

Luke pulled her to him once more just as the music ended and the band struck up a new tune. "You up for a waltz?" he asked, brow raised in skepticism as though he didn't quite believe it was a good idea.

"I'm up for anything you are. Just make sure you get the steps right."

He narrowed his gaze. "Just make sure you follow, or we'll both end up on the floor."

"Fine."

In spite of her determination to remain rigid, Laney's anger sifted from her almost immediately, and she felt the tension leave her shoulders. Enjoying the feel of Luke's strong hand cupping her waist, she closed her eyes, allowing herself to be swept away by the music. Luke spun her around the room without missing a beat.

A soft, contented sigh escaped her lips.

At Luke's sharp intake of breath, Laney opened her eyes. He stared down at her, his green eyes serious and searching. Laney's pulse quickened as his gaze moved across her face, then settled on her lips.

He leaned forward. "Let's get out of here," he said, his voice low against her ear.

Laney shivered from the tickle of his breath, and wordlessly she nodded. She barely noticed the other dancers or the people huddled around the refreshment table as Luke ushered her outside and behind a nearby tree. He leaned back against the oak and took her hands in his as they faced each other.

"What's happening between us, Laney?"

At a loss for words, Laney stared into his dear face, joy invading the very depths of her soul.

He pulled her closer. "I can't sleep for thinking about you and that kiss. What did you do to me?"

A lump lodged deep in Laney's throat, cutting off any reply.

"If you don't stop looking at me like that and say something . . ." Luke growled. He released her hands and pulled her into the circle of his arms. Even before his head descended, Laney knew she was about to be kissed.

His lips brushed against hers once . . . twice — soft and achingly sweet. Laney moved closer as his arms tightened. He pressed his forehead against hers. "My Laney, why didn't I know I've been in love with you all these years?"

Giving her no chance to answer, Luke captured her lips once more.

"Yuck!"

Laney tore herself away from Luke and turned to Tarah's oldest boy, Little D, named for Papa Dell. He sneered in disgust as he observed them.

"I found 'em, Pa!" He turned toward the barn.

"Little D, wait!"

Laney cringed as he hollered, "Uncle Luke's kissing Laney!"

"Get back over here, then, and give them some privacy." Anthony's amused voice brought heat to Laney's cheeks.

"Yuck!" Little D repeated, then took off lickety-split.

Still imprisoned in Luke's iron grip, Laney turned her gaze back to his teasing eyes. He grinned down at her. "Guess I'll have to marry you now that the whole town knows I've been stealing kisses behind the kissing tree."

As usual, the appropriate quip eluded her. "You will?" she whispered.

All traces of teasing fled his expression. "I was just getting around to asking."

"You were?"

"What do you say?"

Yes, yes, yes. The words remained stuck in her throat.

"What? Don't you want to marry me?"

At the hurt expression in his eyes, Laney found her tongue. "I can't imagine marrying anyone else. I just can't believe you're really asking."

A grin spread across Luke's face. With a loud whoop, he snatched her up, spinning her around until she laughed and beat lightly on his broad shoulders.

He set her on her feet. "Do you mean it?"

"Do you?"

"You bet I do."

"Then so do I."

He dipped his head and kissed her again,

leaving her senses reeling by the time he pulled away.

"What do you say to a late winter wedding?" Luke asked. "We'll head west as soon as we can hook up with a wagon train in the spring. We'll be in Oregon by the fall of the year and stake our claim. By the following spring, we'll be ready to start a herd of our own."

Laney's stomach sank to her toes as she watched Luke grow more excited with each word he spoke. "What do you mean, you want to go west, Luke? I haven't heard you mention it since we were still in school. I — I thought you gave up such notions after you started working with your pa."

Luke kissed her hard, then pulled back with a grin. "I've never stopped wanting to go. With you at my side, we'll raise a herd even larger than my pa's."

Laney jerked away from his arms. "So this moving west is all about proving you can outdo your pa? That's just dumb, Luke. And you're dumb for thinking of it."

The line of Luke's jaw tightened. "That's not it. I don't want to build on another man's foundation. I want to make my own way and leave a real legacy to my own son or daughter." Gently he took her hand. "*Our* sons or daughters."

Forcing her gaze from his, Laney turned her back, knowing she'd never be able to say what must be said if she faced him. "I'll bet that's what Papa Dell thought, too. He'd build a herd and leave a real legacy for his sons. Only Sam decided to be a doctor, you're leaving, and Jack and Will are too young to be any real help. If you go, what's your pa going to do? You should wait until Jack is old enough to take over, at least. That'll only be two more years."

Luke shook his head. "Jack's been reading law in Tom Kirkpatrick's office. He's convinced he wants to become an attorney. Pa's offered to send him to Harvard when he passes the last of his courses at the town school."

Laney spun back around. "Then you'll just have to wait until Will grows up. That's only seven or eight more years. You wouldn't even be thirty years old yet."

"By then all the land will be gone! Besides, my pa has plenty of hired hands, just like he did before Sam and I were old enough to help out around the ranch. Just like we will in Oregon."

"It's not the same. It's going to break his heart to see you go."

Luke took her hands in his once more. "Laney, honey, families move off from each other all the time. It's the way of the world. They'll miss us, of course, just like we'll miss them; but we can come back for a visit every two or three years, and Pa and Ma can visit us."

With grim determination, Laney pulled her hands away and planted them firmly on her hips. She shook her head decisively. "Not 'us,' Luke. I'm sorry to go back on my word about marrying you, but I'd rather swallow a live tadpole than move off to *Oregon.* I like it right here in Harper. Besides, now that my brother is marrying Josie Raney, he'll be moving to Virginia as pastor of his own church."

A sickened expression covered Luke's face. "What does Ben have to do with whether or not you marry me?"

So disappointed was she at the unexpected turn of events, Laney didn't even attempt to be patient. "Don't you know anything? Every preacher alive has a passel of young'uns, and they never have enough money to feed themselves, let alone enough to pack them all onto a train to go off visiting a long-lost sister. I'd never see him again."

"We'll work it out. Won't you at least consider it?"

Squaring her shoulders, Laney forced

back the tears tickling her throat. "No, I won't. Ben's all I have in the world, and I won't take a chance on never seeing him again. Besides, ten ladies ordered gowns tonight that have to be ready in time for the Christmas ball. After they pay me, I'll have enough for a down payment on the old soddy."

Luke's mouth dropped open. "You mean you aim to buy the soddy you lived in when you and your pa and Ben first came to Harper?"

"That's right. I've been saving every penny from sewing and working your pa's ranch for the last two years." Laney lifted her chin stubbornly. "Mr. Garner is selling for a right fair price, and he's willing to carry the note himself if I come up with a big enough down payment to prove I'm serious about it. He's selling me five acres to boot, and I can buy more as my own herd grows." She gasped as a wonderful idea flooded her mind. "Luke!"

Luke shook his head. "Don't even suggest it, Laney."

"But why? We'd still be starting our own herd. Only it would be here and not off somewhere away from the family. This is perfect." Laney beamed up at him, then, as emotions got the better of her, there didn't seem anything to do but throw her arms around his neck. So that's what she did. "Tarah was right, as usual," she said over his shoulder. "I don't mind sharing my money with the right man. But don't take to getting liquored up, Luke, or I'll have to hide every cent from you, and I'd never give it up even if you beat me to a bloody pulp."

He gave an exasperated sigh. "You know I'd never take a drink or hit you."

Laney clasped him more tightly around the neck. "Then it's all settled."

Luke's large, steady hands encircled her wrists and pulled her away from him. "I don't want to stay in Harper. I'd always be the 'St. John boy following in his father's footsteps.' Out West I can be my own man. Can't you understand how important that is to me?"

"So you just ask a girl to marry you and then take it back?" Anger burned inside Laney as realization struck her.

"I'm not taking anything back. I'm just saying if you want to marry me, you'll have to go west, because that's where I'm headed next spring."

"Who says I want to marry you, anyway? I wouldn't marry you even if you was stayin' in Harper." Disappointment loosened her tongue and caused her to revert to her

39

childhood speech. "I'd rather marry red-faced ol' Clyde and raise all five of his poor, motherless children — even if he ain't much of a dancer — than have to marry you."

"That suits me just fine."

"Fine!"

"We might as well head back inside, then," Luke said, taking her by the elbow.

Laney jerked away. "Turn your back so I can get out of this skirt."

"What?"

"The skirt. I can't ride home with it on, now, can I?"

Luke shook his head and turned his back. "I don't know why you bother putting it on over britches, anyway. Everyone knows what you're wearing underneath."

Staring at Luke's back, Laney slipped off the skirt and wadded it into a ball. She tucked it under her arm. "All right. You can look now. Tarah and Anthony take too much criticism over me wearing britches, though it seems more indecent to me for everyone to be thinking about what I'm wearing under my skirt than for me to just wear the britches out in the first place."

"When you put it that way . . ."

She shrugged. "Doesn't make much sense, but I guess to some people, as long as they don't have to *see* what's underneath, it

40

doesn't make them uncomfortable knowing what's there."

"I guess."

Still smarting from the disappointing evening, Laney stepped toward the hitching post to get Colby. "Anyway, tell Tarah I rode on home," she said over her shoulder.

Luke grabbed her arm and spun her around to face him. "You're not going by yourself."

"You don't tell me what to do! If I want to ride home by myself, I will!"

"Fine, you stubborn-headed mule. See if I care." Too angry to speak, Laney spun around and headed for her horse. Tears of disappointment forced their way down her cheeks despite her best efforts to keep them at bay.

Who wanted to marry that big, dumb . . . dumb . . . Well, who wanted to, anyway?

Luke quickly stepped inside the barn, knowing it would take Laney no time at all to get saddled and hightail it to the edge of town. Normally the short ride wouldn't cause concern, but after seeing the WANTED poster the sheriff hung up in Tucker's Mercantile just that afternoon, Luke worried for Laney's safety. Her no-account pa had not been seen anywhere near Harper

41

for years, but according to the poster, he and a couple of men he rode with had robbed the home of a wealthy businessman in Topeka not two weeks ago. Topeka was too close to Harper for Luke's comfort. He'd feel better if the man were clear across the country. If Mr. Jenkins decided to head this direction and look up his children, he'd be able to spot Laney like a red barn in a green field. She hadn't changed all that much in eight years. She still wore britches except for in public places, and her hair hung in a thick, dark blond braid down the center of her back. No bigger than a twelve-year-old boy, she would be an easy target if someone wanted to grab her. She'd put up a good fight, but her size would be a disadvantage.

"Where's Laney?" Tarah's eyes twinkled with teasing. "Little D is completely disgusted that you've joined the ranks of the kissing men, Uncle Luke. I don't believe he will ever trust you again."

Luke felt his ears heat up. "He can lay his fears to rest. I just came back over to the other side."

She chuckled and rubbed her protruding stomach. "That didn't take long."

"That's what I came to tell you. Laney and I had words, and she took off for home.

I'm going to make sure she makes it all right."

"You two are hopeless." In spite of her words, Tarah's lips twitched. "It's not that far, Luke. I'm sure she'll be fine. Why don't you stay and enjoy the dance?"

"I'll explain it to you some other time. I have to go."

Without waiting for a reply, Luke left. He quickly mounted his horse and headed toward the parsonage. To his relief, a soft glow came from inside the stable. He dismounted and tethered Rusty to the hitching post outside the church. Striding purposefully toward the stable, Luke determined not to be dissuaded from his mission to see her safely inside the house. As he approached, the sound of wrenching sobs stopped him in his tracks.

Laney! He had never heard her cry before hadn't really thought her capable of shedding tears. Compassion mingled with his own disappointment. He longed to hold her . . . to comfort them both. Without thinking, Luke stepped inside the musty stable. Pungent odors of manure and fresh hay assailed his senses. "Laney?"

She glanced up sharply, swiping her gingham sleeve across her face. "What are you doing here? I thought I told you I didn't need you following me home."

"I just wanted to be sure you were safe."

"I'm just fine. And don't think I'm crying because of you, because I'm not. I — I just . . . Well, I'm just . . ." She kicked at the wood stall where her horse munched on hay. "It's none of your business why I'm crying, so just go home and don't you dare tell anyone, or I'll flat out deny it."

"I wouldn't dream of telling."

"Make sure you don't," she warned, obviously unappeased by his smile.

"I need to tell you something."

Laney sniffed. "Please, Luke," she said wearily. "I don't think I can take any more of your news tonight."

"It's important."

Her chest heaved with a long-suffering sigh. "All right, but make it fast so I can be in bed before the family gets back from the dance. I don't feel like dealing with Little D."

Luke told her about the poster. Her expression changed from sadness to horror as she listened, her eyes widening in fright.

"Do you think he'll try to come back here and get me to help him hide from the law?"

"I don't know, honey. But you need to be on the lookout for him, just in case. I'll be watching, too. Try not to go off riding by yourself."

"I can't stay locked up like a prisoner." Determinedly Laney grabbed the lantern from its nail. She walked with purpose to the doors and glanced expectantly at Luke. He followed, wishing the events of the night had not unfolded as they had. They should be celebrating their betrothal with family and friends right now — not standing outside in the cold autumn night, about to get into another argument because of Laney's stubbornness.

"You have to be more careful. No other woman in this town would gallivant the way you do without a chaperone."

A snicker escaped her. "Tarah rides out to the ranch all the time by herself, and Anthony doesn't mind."

"All right. I should clarify that only the women in my family would ride around alone."

"If Pa wants to find me, he will — whether I'm hiding out or riding alone on the prairie. I'm not going to hole up like some coward. I just can't." They reached the parsonage steps, and Laney turned. "Thank you for the concern, Luke. I appreciate it. But I've always looked after myself. I'll be all right. Good night."

Luke watched her step inside and close

the door, knowing there was nothing he could say. He wished he could go back and relive the past couple of hours. He had added to Laney's hurt tonight by asking her to marry him before he shared his plans to move west. He had been too caught up in her large doelike eyes and her soft, rosy lips and wasn't thinking clearly.

Still, if a woman loved a man enough, wouldn't she be willing to go with him? Luke pondered the question as he rode the few miles out to the St. John ranch. The thought tightened his stomach. He wished for all he was worth he had never teased her on the way home from Abilene. Then she wouldn't have kissed him, and their friendship would never have been distorted. But it was too late for regrets. No matter how many miles separated them, Luke would never forget the joy of holding her in his arms or the sweetness of her kiss.

CHAPTER 3

Laney stared at the wanted poster on the wall in Tucker's Mercantile. The man in the sketch looked older and thinner than she remembered, but there was no denying the cold eyes staring back at her. Memories she'd thought were long buried assaulted her. Laney shivered. Pa was back.

"Afternoon, Laney."

She jumped as Mr. Tucker entered from the back room. Dragging her gaze from the poster, Laney stepped up to the counter, trying to pretend nonchalance.

Tucker nodded toward the wall. "Thought he looked an awful lot like yer pa, even if he is goin' by the name Hiram Jones."

"Yeah, it's him." Laney lifted her shoulders in an it-don't-bother-me-none shrug.

Tucker raised his gray, bushy brows. "You just mind yerself and be careful. Ya hear?"

"I can take care of myself." Laney lifted her chin. Why did everyone think she needed to be protected?

Tucker let out an unpleasant snort. "Yer barely big enough to look over this counter without standing on your tippy toes, gal. What makes you think you can hold yer own against someone as big and mean as yer pa?"

Laney pulled back her sheepskin coat and revealed the gun belt hanging from her boyishly small hips, over her new wool skirt. "I'd say this just about evens the odds, wouldn't you?"

The old man's eyes narrowed. "Now see here. Does yer family know yer totin' a Colt?"

Letting the coat drop back into place, Laney met Tucker's gaze head-on. "No. And don't you go blabbing, either. You'll just make Tarah worry, and she doesn't need to be doing that in her condition."

"I ain't makin' no promises, missy, so don't try to bully me. If I feel the need to spill yer little secret, I will."

Laney glared at the old codger. Tucker wasn't one to back down from a fight. Even though he'd become a Christian years ago, he was still as formidable as ever.

"Have it your way, then." She rose up on her toes and leaned her elbows on the tall counter. "Anthony said you wanted to see me."

48

Tucker nodded. "That's right. I got a proposition fer you."

Laney's eyes widened, and she inwardly retreated. Was Mr. Tucker losing his mind? "Mr. Tucker, maybe you should think about this some more before you —"

The storekeeper shook his head. "Nope. Got my mind made up. Yer just what I been lookin' fer."

Stepping away from the counter, Laney glowered. "I like you fine, Tucker. You're a real hard worker and nice enough when you take a notion to be, but I ain't marrying up with a man old enough to be my pa's uncle!"

Brows knit together, Mr. Tucker turned red beneath his scraggly whiskers. "Are you goin' soft in the head? I ain't askin' you to marry up with me, gal!"

Mortified, Laney lowered her gaze as heat suffused her cheeks. "What other proposition did you have in mind?"

"What are you two yelling at each other about?"

Neither Mr. Tucker nor Laney had heard the bell above the door signaling Luke's entrance into the mercantile.

Laney stared at the floor. "Nothing," she muttered.

"Just a misunderstanding," Mr. Tucker

confirmed.

Laney could have kissed the old coot for sparing her more humiliation in front of Luke.

"I was just telling Laney here that I got a proposition fer her."

"What proposition?" Luke asked. His eyes narrowed, and Laney knew instinctively he had made the same assumption she had. The thought warmed her.

"A *business* proposition."

Laney's ears perked up. "What'd you have in mind?"

"How'd you like to work for me, sewing dresses for the store?"

"And split my profit?"

" 'Course."

Laney's brow furrowed. "Why would I want to do that? I get to keep all my money when I drum up my own business."

"Yeah, but how much business do you drum up?"

Laney drew herself up to her full height. "I got myself ten orders at the dance last week."

"Party dresses?"

"That's right."

"Well, that ain't what I'm talkin' about, missy. So how's about you closin' yer trap and hearin' me out?"

Smarting under the reprimand, Laney sized him up for a minute. Mr. Tucker wouldn't suggest something that wouldn't benefit her. He was like a grand old uncle. "I'm listening."

Luke shifted his weight and leaned against the counter. Laney felt his nearness as keenly as if he had embraced her. She cleared her throat and tried to concentrate on Mr. Tucker's voice.

"Now them hoity-toity ladies movin' to Harper from the cities come in here all the time lookin' fer ready-made dresses. I'm losin' business if they order from them books." He leaned forward and pointed a gnarled finger toward her face. "If you and me was to partner up, we'd both stand to make a profit."

"I understand that, Mr. Tucker, but why shouldn't I just get my business straight from them?"

He sent her a scowl fierce enough to intimidate a grizzly. Laney's eyes grew wide, and she stepped back. "It ain't right for you to take my idea and go lookin' fer business after I'm the one that brought it up in the first place. Ain't living with that preacher all these years taught you nothin', gal?"

Luke chuckled. "He has a point."

Laney turned the full force of her glare

upon him, then focused her attention once more on Mr. Tucker.

Luke was right; Tucker did have a point. Still, she could have kicked herself for not thinking of advertising for her own business in the first place. "All right. Let's hear your terms."

She listened carefully and had to admit she would save the funds to buy her soddy and start a herd much quicker if she accepted the proposal.

"Throw in the dress goods and I might consider it."

Tucker stared at her as though she had lost her mind. "You expect me to provide the dress goods *and* split the profits fifty-fifty?"

Laney shrugged. "I have to do all the work. Seems fair to me."

Tucker squinted at her as if considering. "All right," he grumbled. "But it sounds like highway robbery to me."

Elated, Laney nodded, trying not to glow with victory. She'd never expected Tucker to give in so easily. "And I broke the handle on my shears last week, so I'll need a new pair."

Tucker gave her a wry grin. "You can pay for those, can't you?"

Luke chuckled. "Seems to me that's the

least you can do, Laney."

Grudgingly Laney handed over the money. "All right. You willin' to put all this in writing?"

Laney winced as Mr. Tucker's mouth turned down in indignation. "What do you take me fer? Some thief? We got a witness right here." He jerked his thumb toward Luke.

"That's not what I mean. I want to show Mr. Garner proof of a steady income so I can get my soddy. I won't have room to work at Anthony and Tarah's with all those kids running around."

Appeased, Mr. Tucker nodded. "Reckon I can do that."

Twenty minutes later, with signed proof of a steady income, Laney strode from the mercantile and headed for her horse.

Luke followed. "Congratulations. Looks like you're getting what you wanted."

"Looks that way." Then why did she feel so empty when she gazed at the familiar freckled face staring back at her? "How about you? You told your ma and pa about your plans?"

Luke's jaw tightened. "Not yet."

"It'll be all right, Luke. You have a right to be your own man. Your pa will understand that."

A short laugh lifted his shoulders. "But you can't understand it?"

"I just don't see why you'd want to leave your family. If you'd stay here and help me start my herd . . ."

"Your herd?"

"Well, it would be ours. Yours and mine. If you'd stop being so stubborn about letting me share it with you."

Luke smiled at her. "I have money saved. I could help you buy the soddy and start the herd."

Hope lifted Laney's drooping spirits.

"But that's not the point. I want to go west and be my own man."

"But, Luke, if you stay here and we got mar—" Laney stopped. She would not beg.

Luke's brow arched. "If we got married?" He reached for her hand, sending warmth through her belly. Luke's gaze searched hers, drawing Laney in until she was certain. "Don't go put that money down on the soddy, Laney. Marry me. Come west and let's build a life together. Don't you see how good it would be between us?"

Looking into Luke's emerald green eyes and remembering the warmth of his kisses, Laney almost relented. But reason prevailed. She snatched her hand away. "I can't do it, Luke. I just can't." Quickly she mounted her horse. She stared down at him. "You got your plans, and I got mine. They just don't match up, that's all." Without giving him a chance to respond, she whipped her horse around and headed off toward Mr. Garner's property. She knew if she stayed any longer, she would fall into Luke's arms and never leave them. But Harper was home. Tarah and Anthony and their brood were home. How could she give them up? No. This way was for the best. Luke would go to Oregon and fulfill his dreams, and she would stay here and fulfill hers.

It was for the best. . . .

Luke drove in the last stake for the new fence and stepped back to wipe the sweat from his brow. "There," he said, taking the proffered canteen from his pa. "If that doesn't keep Ol' Angus in his own pasture, nothing will."

He took a swig of the tepid water, wiped his mouth with the back of his arm, and screwed the lid back on the canteen.

Pa leaned his weight against the newly repaired fence. "I thought I'd go ahead and buy a new bull next year in Abilene." He stared at the bull with a troubled expression. "Ol' Angus has just about worn out his usefulness, and he's getting meaner than a grizzly from what I can tell. I'm worried he'll get loose and gore a young'un walking home from school."

Luke nodded, clenching his teeth to refrain from mentioning that he'd been suggesting that very thing for the past year. The aging bull had knocked this same fence down twice in the past six months trying to get at a passing rider or someone walking through the north field. If Pa had listened in the first place, they wouldn't have had to waste time making the repairs.

"Reckon you already knew that about Ol' Angus, huh?"

Luke stared off into the blue horizon. "I reckon." What else could he say?

"I should have listened to you." Pa kept his own gaze fixed beyond the brown field.

Luke knew what the admission had cost his pa. He remained silent, sensing there was more to this conversation than Ol' Angus's foul temper.

Pa cleared his throat. "I know I've been pretty hard on you, son. There were times when I could have taken your advice and should have but didn't. I guess my pride got the best of me. It's not easy to admit my son might know more than I do about ranching." A chuckle rumbled his chest, and he coughed, then pulled out his handkerchief and blew his nose.

"You taking a cold, Pa?"

"Must be. But don't go telling your ma, or she'll have me sitting in front of the fire sipping hot tea and all wrapped up in a quilt."

Luke grinned. His pa carried on, but everyone knew he loved Ma's attention. Marrying late in life, Luke's stepmother, Cassidy, had years of nurturing to catch up on, and she babied anyone who would allow it. Luke could scarcely remember a time when she hadn't been a part of their lives. His memories of his own ma were misty, and except for the daguerreotype sitting on Tarah's mantel, he wouldn't remember her at all. Cassidy had filled that empty space long ago, and he couldn't love her more if she truly were his mother.

Pa sneezed, drawing Luke's focus back to the present. "I reckon we oughtta head back to the house. Ma'll tan my hide if I let you catch pneumonia."

"In a minute." Pa turned to face him. "I want to talk to you about something."

At Pa's serious tone, a gnawing sensation nearly overwhelmed Luke's stomach. Had he somehow caught wind of Luke's plans to move west? Luke knew it was time to come clean, but he dreaded the conversation.

"What is it, Pa?"

"I've decided it's time you start taking on more responsibility around the ranch. I've never had a manager before, but I'm offering you the position, son."

"Manager? You have a foreman."

Pa shook his head. "I need someone to oversee the ins and outs of the ranching — not just to watch over the hands — do the hiring and firing, accounts, keep track of the buying and selling. That sort of thing."

"But you do that."

"I have. And now I'm ready to hand it over. Sam never was interested in ranching, and of course Jack is headed for college in a couple of years. Will might enjoy ranching, but you'll get the lion's share when I'm gone. Thought you might like a chance to put some of your ideas into practice without me standing over you telling you no all the time. You can run the ranch any way you see fit."

Luke tried to make sense of Pa's words, but he couldn't quite wrap his mind around the truth of the matter. "But if I take over for you, what are you going to do?"

Pa chortled, then coughed again. "Don't worry, I'll be around, getting in the way. I'm just ready to hand over the responsibility." He peered closer at Luke, his brow creased. "I thought this would be good news. Am I wrong?"

Just say it. You can't take on a position like this and then up and quit come spring. Pa deserves to know the truth so he can make other plans.

"The fact is, Pa . . ." Luke cleared his throat, then braced himself for whatever reaction Pa would give. "The fact is that I got other plans."

"What kind of plans?" He sounded hurt, confused, and worried all at the same time.

Luke nearly relented, but he knew he couldn't. The thought of running the St. John ranch for the rest of his life left a bitter taste in his mouth. He had to make it on his own.

"I don't mean to sound ungrateful. I love the ranch; you know that. I'll do whatever I can to help — until I move west in the spring."

Pa drew in a long, slow breath, the kind he always drew when trying to maintain control. "When did you decide this?"

"I've always planned to, but lately it's all I can think about." Despite the intensity of the moment, Luke's excitement rose. "I've been saving every penny to start my own herd." Luke's plans spilled from his lips like water over a fall. When he stopped and glanced at his pa, the man's eyes were moist, but a smile lifted his lips.

"I see you've thought this through." Pa clapped him on the shoulder and strode toward his gray mare. "Let's get back. I promised your ma we'd be back in plenty of time to clean up and get to church." With a sad smile, he mounted the horse.

Luke's stomach clenched. He climbed into Rusty's saddle and urged the roan forward. "Pa, I could stay on until Will's old enough to take over." He heard his voice but couldn't quite believe he'd made the offer.

"I appreciate that, son. But it'll be a few years yet before your little brother is old enough to break a horse, much less run a ranch. But that's my concern, not yours. I won't have it said I held back any of my children from their dreams. Sam's a doctor, Jack's going to practice law, your sister is married with a brood of her own, and they're a happy bunch." He gave a short laugh. "Even little Laney is doing just what she's been bragging she'd do for the past five years. She's got herself that little soddy and plans to start a herd of her own in a couple of years."

Pain stabbed at Luke's heart. Laney had made herself pretty scarce the past three weeks. He'd heard from Tarah and other female members of his family that she was sewing her fingers to the bone and happy as a pig in slop to be doing it in her own home. It stung his pride to know she was so happy without him. "So I heard," he said, trying to keep his voice even.

"Don't you think your happiness is just as important to me? If you want to go off and make it on your own like I did when I came here to Kansas, I won't be the one to try and stop you."

Relief flowed over Luke like a cool summer shower. "You're not mad?"

"Nope. I just assumed because you have ranching in your blood like me that you'd be content to stay on and take over for me. I should have asked you what you wanted instead of taking it for granted. I'm sorry you found it so hard to share your dreams with me, son. Cassidy is right. I can be mighty thickheaded at times."

"You're not the only one."

Riding back to the house next to his pa, Luke felt a kinship like he'd never felt before, even though they'd worked side by side for as long as Luke could remember. His insides quivered with excitement now that the last barrier to his dream had been knocked over. Only one thing would have made everything perfect: if Laney would share the dream with him; but she had made her choice and had found happiness in fulfilling her own plans. He had to accept that and move on without her. But how did one function when he felt incomplete — as though he were only half a man?

CHAPTER 4

Laney suppressed a yawn while she waited just inside the church doors for the crowd surrounding Anthony to diminish. She eyed the side door, wishing she could slip out unnoticed and head for her little soddy.

With a gnawing sense of dread, she envisioned the enormity of the task awaiting her when she arrived home. She still had one Christmas gown to finish for Mrs. Thomas and one for Mr. Tucker's mercantile before next Saturday. How she was going to get everything done, she'd never know.

"Laney, honey, you okay?"

Laney turned at the sound of Mama Cassidy's voice. The older woman's worried tone warmed Laney. Tired as she was, she would like nothing better than to lay her head on Mama Cassidy's shoulder and close her eyes for ten minutes.

"I'm all right. Just a little tired." She gave what she hoped to be a reassuring smile;

but from the deepening skepticism on Mama Cassidy's face, she knew she hadn't been very convincing.

"You have circles under your eyes." She cupped Laney's chin. Mama Cassidy's green-eyed gaze studied every line of her face, then swept over the rest of her. "And you've obviously lost weight. My guess is that you haven't been sleeping or eating since you moved out on your own."

Unable to deny it, Laney shifted her weight from one booted foot to the other and dropped her gaze to the wooden floor.

Mama Cassidy gave her a one-armed hug and a gentle smile. "That's all right. You'll eat at the picnic and take a nap afterwards. You'll be sick if you don't take care of yourself."

Clearing her throat, Laney gathered her courage to broach the topic of the picnic. She would need to tread lightly if she was to get out of it without too much outcry from her large adoptive family. "To be honest, I —"

"Mama, you look lovely this morning."

Laney stopped as Tarah joined them, carrying little Olive in her arms. She brushed a kiss on her stepmother's cheek. When she turned to greet Laney, the smile faded from her lips, to be quickly replaced with an indignant frown.

"Laney Jenkins, you promised you'd get more rest."

"I did," Laney mumbled.

Tarah's gaze traveled over her. "Not much, from the looks of you. Have you been eating the food I've been sending over, or is it going to waste?"

"I eat some of it." A few bites here and there, when her fingers weren't too busy to pick up a fork.

"Not much, I'd say." The thump of a cane hitting the wooden floor accompanied a sharp voice.

Laney inwardly groaned. If Granny Ellen joined the hovering women, she might as well forget about skipping the picnic. With as sweet a smile as she could muster, she faced the women, feeling as though she were standing before a jury — only these jurors had already made up their minds. She was guilty of not taking care of herself. If she didn't control the situation, not only would they force her to attend the picnic; they'd take turns standing over her to make sure she was eating to their satisfaction.

"You all are dear to worry so much about me. I promise to take better care of myself. I declare, sewing for Mr. Tucker has me busier than a fox in a henhouse." Laney cleared her throat. "As a matter of fact —"

"Harrumph." Granny Ellen narrowed her gaze. "Don't try to sweet-talk your way out of the picnic today. I can see plain as day you want to go home and sew." She thumped her cane on the floor for emphasis. "I'll not have a member of my family working on the Lord's Day, so you get that notion right out of your head. And don't go blaming it all on Mr. Tucker, either. He would never approve of your working on the Lord's Day! So there, girlie."

"Laney!" Tarah's eyes widened. "You know very well it wouldn't be the same without you. No one would have a bit of fun."

Fully prepared to put up a fight, Laney glanced at the determined faces and changed her mind. If she knew Tarah and the rest of the St. Johns, they'd hog-tie her and throw her into the back of a wagon before allowing her to skip the picnic. And as much as she'd like to be irritated at the whole situation, something about the reminder that so many people loved her warmed Laney to her toes.

With an exaggerated sigh of defeat, she nodded. "All right. I'll go to the picnic. But only for a little while. At sundown I have to get back to sewing, or I'll never finish."

■ ■ ■ ■

Relief coursed through Luke at the sight of Laney riding alongside Tarah and Anthony's wagon. He hadn't been at all sure she'd even show up to the picnic. As she drew nearer, alarm shot through him. She looked downright worn to a frazzle. When she dismounted, he noticed the usual spring in her step had been replaced by a weary stride.

He moved quickly to her side. "You look like you haven't slept in a week."

"So I've been told," she said dryly. She grabbed a basket of food from the back of Tarah's wagon and headed for the picnic site.

Luke fell into step beside her. "You're working too hard."

She glanced up, and alarm seized Luke at the dark smudges beneath her eyes.

"It's not possible to work too hard." She stifled a yawn. "Hard work gets you where you want to go in life."

"Working too hard gets you dead, or sick at least. Give me that basket."

Alarm clenched his throat like a hangman's noose when she let out a weary sigh of relief upon relinquishing the load. He stopped in his tracks.

She halted beside him. "What's wrong?"

"You. You're worn to a frazzle. I'm talking to Tucker about getting you some help, and you're going to have to stop accepting so many orders."

"Oh, Luke, mind your own business." Turning, Laney ambled away without putting up a fight, which only fueled Luke's concern. He went after her, took her by the arm, and turned her to face him. "I think you should have Sam check you over."

A slow smile tilted her lips, making Luke wish he were free to swoop her up in his arms and force her to rest.

"I'm not sick, Lukey."

The childhood pet name used to make him mad back when he was a boy, but now he delighted in the familiarity, accepting the name as an endearment from Laney's lips.

She passed her slender hand across her forehead. "I'm just tired. Once I finish this order for Mr. Tucker, I'm going to take some time to rest. I promise. Now come on, they're waiting for that food."

"Laney, come play ball with us!"

Little D's shrill voice cut through the air just as Luke was about to insist Laney go lay down in the back of the wagon until Cassidy called them to eat. He addressed his nephew instead. "Laney's too tired to play today."

"Aw! Who's going to pitch?" Little D ran to them.

"Find someone else," Luke replied firmly.

Little D kicked the ground. "But no one else can get it over the plate!"

"Too bad. Laney needs to rest."

Laney planted her hands on her hips. "Wait a minute. Who said I was too tired to play ball?"

"It's obvious," Luke replied.

"You don't speak for me, Luke St. John. If I want to pitch for the kids, I will!"

She draped her arm over Little D's shoulders. "Come on, let's go."

Helplessly Luke watched them go. He shook his head. Laney would be stubborn enough to play with the kids just to show him he couldn't boss her around.

Turning, he headed to the picnic spot and handed the basket to Tarah.

"What are we going to do about that girl, Luke?" she asked, concern edging her voice.

"There's not much we can do. She's as stubborn as a mule in a briar patch and kicks twice as hard when anyone tries to help her. I say let her work herself into an early grave. It'll serve her right."

"Honestly," Tarah huffed. "You know full

well you don't mean that. When you want to be reasonable, we'll talk."

Luke opened his mouth to let her know just how much he meant what he'd said, but a cry from the ballplayers drew his attention.

"Look at her fly!"

"Run, Laney!"

Luke walked toward the game, shaking his head. That Laney just had to go and hit a home run to prove him wrong. He grinned in spite of himself. Maybe she wasn't as frail as she appeared after all.

She rounded second base, flashing him a triumphant smile. Just as quickly, the smile faded and she slowed to a walk, her hand pressed against her forehead.

"Laney?"

A look of bewilderment clouded her face, and in a flash, she crumpled to the ground. Luke's mouth went dry. He broke into a trot and quickly closed the distance between them.

"Little D, go get Sam!" He knelt beside her and took her limp hand in his, breathing a sigh of relief at the steady beat of her pulse. Laney had always been tiny, even for a woman; but lying on the ground, her skin pale, her lashes brushing her cheeks, she looked like a doll. Running a thumb gently

70

across the back of her hand, Luke prayed a silent prayer. *Let her be all right, Lord. As much as I'd like to strangle her at times, I couldn't stand it if something were seriously wrong.*

A shadow fell across Laney's still form. Luke glanced up to find his brother standing over them. "Move out of the way, Luke," Sam commanded. "Let me take a look."

Reluctantly Luke released her hand and stepped back.

"She's exhausted," Sam announced after a short examination. "But I think that's all that's wrong."

By now the family had encircled the unconscious girl. "That settles it," Mama Cassidy announced with an air of finality. "Laney is coming home with us. Luke, carry her to the wagon, and we'll take her home right now."

"No, Mama," Tarah said. "She should come home with Anthony and me. Put her in our wagon, Luke."

Mama Cassidy set her lips into a grim line. "Honey, I know you love Laney, but she wouldn't get any rest at all with the children running around."

Luke scooped Laney into his arms, wondering which of the strong-willed women would relent.

A sigh escaped Tarah's lips. "You're right, of course." She nodded to Luke. "Take her to Ma and Pa's wagon. We'll be over later to check on her."

Luke glanced down into Laney's pale face, and his heart lurched. Who would be there to take care of her after he was gone?

Laney snuggled deeper into the fluffy goose feather mattress and sighed. She felt more rested than she had in ages. Her mouth stretched into a wide yawn, then curved into a contented smile. With a start, her eyes flew open. Rest could only mean one thing: She'd slept too long, and Tucker's dresses wouldn't be done in time.

Glancing around the familiar room, confusion settled over Laney. What was she doing in Granny Ellen's room at the ranch, anyhow? Then the memories rushed back to haunt her. She remembered running the bases and feeling fuzzy in the head. A gasp escaped her throat. Horror of horrors! She'd fainted! Like a girl — a weak-kneed, eyelash-batting, dress-wearing girl! She'd never live this down in a million and a half years.

She groaned, picturing the stupid, teasing grin sure to be on Luke's face the next time she saw him — which wouldn't be long, since she was at the ranch.

Throwing back the rose-colored coverlet, she stiffened in resolution. There was no way she'd stand for Luke's insults. Besides, she had a ton of work to do, and she couldn't very well finish those dresses while lying abed.

The sun shone bright outside, so Laney figured she hadn't slept too long. If the family was still at the picnic, she could sneak out and get back to the soddy before anyone could stop her and insist she eat supper or spend the night.

She swung her legs over the side of the bed, and her brows lifted in surprise. When had she changed into a nightdress? Mama Cassidy probably changed her. They must have assumed she would sleep all night. Laney hated to hurt anyone's feelings, but she couldn't take the time to stay here and be pampered, although she had to admit it would have been nice.

Now where were her britches? Hands on her hips, she glanced around the room.

It was a conspiracy! They had brought her here against her wishes and hid all of her clothes so she couldn't go anywhere.

She stomped across to the door and jerked it open. Her scream mingled with Mama Cassidy's as they came face-to-face at the threshold.

"Honestly, Laney, you nearly scared the life right out of me! What are you doing out of bed, anyway?"

"I'm sorry, Mama Cassidy. I didn't know anyone was home from the picnic." Laney waved toward the bedroom. "I need to get home, but I can't find my clothes."

"The picnic?" Cassidy's face lit with amusement. "Laney, honey, you've been sleeping for two days. It's Tuesday afternoon."

"Tuesday?" That just couldn't be! She'd lost two whole days of work!

"I was just getting ready to wake you so you could eat something."

"Oh, Mama Cassidy! I have to get home. I have so much work to do. Please tell me where my clothes are."

"Nonsense." Taking her by her upper arm, Cassidy steered Laney back toward the bed. "You get back under those covers, and I'm going to go warm up some venison stew and biscuits for you."

An upraised hand silenced Laney's protests. "Don't worry about the gowns. Granny and Tarah are working on the two you need to finish this week, and the others can wait until you get home next week."

"Next week! Tarah has plenty to do without taking on my work, too. What is she thinking?"

"She's thinking that the girl she's loved and cared for all these years is so stubborn that instead of asking her family for help, she worked herself sick."

Ashamed, Laney fixed her gaze on her broken fingernails. "I'm sorry," she mumbled. "I didn't mean to worry anyone." Without more protest, Laney allowed herself to be tucked into bed. Mama Cassidy sat beside her and adjusted the coverlet around her shoulders.

"I know you didn't, honey. But after all these years as part of this family, you should know we'd do anything to help one of our own. Your dreams are our dreams, too. We're all so proud of you."

Tears pricked Laney's eyes. How she loved this family! Luke was an idiot to even consider leaving.

Cassidy patted Laney's hand. "You just stay right here and rest while I go get you something to eat."

Unable to argue, Laney nodded. She watched Mama Cassidy leave the room and closed her eyes, drinking in the scents of lemon verbena combined with liniment, which always seemed to cling to Granny Ellen.

She snuggled back down into the comfort

of the fluffy mattress and coverlet and closed her eyes. Immediately the image of Luke standing over her, asking her to marry him, came back to her mind as vividly as if the dance was just yesterday. Before she could push the memory aside, the feel of his arms and the touch of his lips flooded back to torment her.

"Lukey," she whispered. "Why did I have to go and fall in love with a man itching to move out west? We could have been so happy together raising a passel of young'uns right in the middle of this big family. Why can't you just be content with what you've been given?"

Hot tears escaped her closed eyes and slipped down her cheeks. With an angry swipe, she brushed them away. First she'd fainted; now she was crying for no good reason! Loving Luke had turned her into just the sort of woman she'd always held in contempt.

She released a resolute sigh. The fact was, tears or no, she couldn't help loving Luke. And whether she wanted to or not, she would go on loving him forever.

CHAPTER 5

Laney entered her soddy, a smile spread across her face. A contented sigh escaped her lips. *Home.*

Upon further inspection of the room, warmth flooded her cheeks. The house was twice as clean as it had been when she'd left for church the previous Sunday. It didn't take much for Laney to picture Granny clucking and shaking her head while she picked up the clutter.

Shaking off the embarrassment, Laney moved across the room, determined to get in as much work as possible before nightfall — the time she'd promised Mama Cassidy and Tarah that she would stop working, eat a bite of food, and head to bed for a full night's sleep. When her gaze reached the corner of the room where she had set up her work area, her mouth dropped open. Shelves stood before her, reaching from the ceiling to the earthen floor. She tested the smooth wood with her fingertips, marveling at its softness. Her dress goods were folded and arranged on shelves according to fabric. Smaller shelves contained other necessary items such as thread and shears.

"Do you like it?"

Laney spun around, her hand pressed against her heart. "Luke, do you have to sneak up on a person?"

A grin split his face. "Sorry." He inclined his head toward the shelves. "What do you think?"

"What do I think?" She clasped her hands together to keep from making a fool of herself by clapping with delight. "It's the most beautiful thing I've ever seen. Who made it?"

Luke's face reddened, and his Adam's apple bobbed in his neck.

Laney's eyes widened. "You did this?"

"Yeah," he mumbled, then cleared his throat. "Where do you want Granny's trunk?"

"Luke, I don't know what to say. I'm so grateful, I —" She stopped short as her mind registered his last question at the same time she noticed the oak trunk at his feet. "What do you mean, where do I want Granny's trunk?"

"You didn't expect her to come with just

the clothes on her back, did you?" Luke's lips twitched with amusement.

"Luke, what are you talking about? Why is Granny coming?"

He studied her face a moment, bewilderment registering in his own expression. Then he threw back his head and howled with laughter. "They didn't tell you!"

A sense of dread tightened Laney's stomach. "Tell me what? Stop that cackling this minute, or so help me, I'll flatten you."

"Granny is coming tomorrow to stay with you."

Weakness settled in Laney's knees. She grabbed a nearby chair and sat before she lost the ability to stand. "Tell me you're joking," she whispered.

" 'Fraid not," he drawled. "And it's your own fault for making yourself sick."

"How long is she staying? A week?" That sounded fair. After all, Laney had shared her room for a week.

Again, Luke's lips twitched. "Guess again."

"Two?" Laney gulped.

"Laney, Granny's moving in — lock, stock, and barrel."

A groan escaped Laney's throat. "Think it would make a difference if I promise to eat and sleep more?"

"Not a chance. You know Granny; she's convinced that you need her, and she's going to stay here no matter what." He hoisted the trunk across his back. "Where to?" he asked, groaning under the weight.

"Oh, who cares?" she replied, giving him a distracted wave. "Anywhere you can find a spot for it is fine." What difference did it make? This was no longer her home. Granny would move in and take over completely. Laney might as well move back in with Tarah and Anthony for all the freedom she'd have now.

Luke deposited the trunk in a spare corner, then turned. "It might not be so bad. Personally I feel a lot better knowing Granny's going to be here to look after you."

Laney's ire rose. She stood, stretching to her full height. "I don't need anyone looking after me. I can take care of myself."

With a smirk, Luke headed toward the door, then turned and faced her. "I guess I could remind you where you just spent the last week — and why; but knowing you, you'd deny the whole thing just to try to prove a point. Regardless, you'd best get used to the idea. Granny's moving in, and there's nothing you can do about it."

He turned his back and ducked through the doorway. Laney stomped across the room, intending to slam the door behind him; but when she peeked out, she realized he wasn't finished unloading the wagon.

Granny had brought all of her bedding, as well.

"Move back so I can get it through the door. Oh." Luke pulled a bottle out of his pocket. "Granny's liniment."

Tears of condemnation sprang to Laney's eyes. "I'm rotten to the core, Luke. Here I have been thinking about Granny invading my house and taking away my privacy, and really she's the one sacrificing her comfort for me. She'll ache all the time, what with the arthritis in her hip. And you know I'll have to fight her to take my bed and let me take the floor."

Luke reached forward and captured Laney's hand. "The last thing you are is rotten to the core, honey. And I know exactly how you feel. As much as I love our family and thank God for them, sometimes it can feel like you're being smothered."

Laney nodded, still inwardly berating herself for her pathetic lack of loyalty to the family who took her in and loved her as though she were one of their own. She barely noticed when Luke stepped closer, until he was so close she had to look up to meet his gaze.

"Now that you understand how I feel, won't you change your mind and come west with me? We'll have the wide-open range and all the freedom we could possibly want."

Laney glowered, shocked beyond words at the very suggestion. When she recovered her voice, she gave it to him with both barrels blazing. "Luke St. John, how can you even suggest I leave these wonderful people after all they've done for me?"

Luke's jaw dropped open. "Six seconds ago, you were ready to throw poor Granny out on her ear to have your privacy, and now they're too wonderful to leave behind?" He grabbed his Stetson from the table and headed toward the door. "You're crazy!"

Laney stormed after him, but he was already in the wagon before she reached the threshold. "Oh yeah?" she called after him. "Well, you're . . . you're —" *Rats!* He was already driving away. She reared back and slammed the door as hard as she could. Gaining little satisfaction, she kicked at the closest chair.

As pain laced her toes, bringing her back to her senses, Laney felt the heat creep to her cheeks. She had to stop letting Luke rile her so much. Especially after Anthony had just preached a sermon yesterday about a person not sinning even when they are mad as all getout. And she hardly ever got mad at anyone besides Luke. So he pretty much was the only reason she'd sinned in the first place. She knew she had to stop allowing Luke to goad her into getting so angry. Of course, he would be gone in a few months, and that would be the end of that.

Sobered by the last thought, Laney felt her shoulders slump. During the past week, each conversation she had shared with Luke inevitably steered toward the topic of his heading to Oregon. Laney couldn't stop the despair from flooding her at the memory of his green eyes shining with excitement as he spoke of raising his herd and leaving a legacy for his children. His children. Pain knifed through Laney. Children he would share with another woman. White-hot hatred flared inside her toward that other woman — the nameless, faceless woman who would share Luke's dream and win his love away from Laney.

Suddenly she hurried to her bed and knelt. She planted her elbows on the mattress and closed her eyes. Unable to bring herself to talk aloud in the empty room, she silently petitioned God.

I know You're up there looking out for me, God, just like You have ever since I was just

a tyke. I want to thank You again for not let-
ting me grow up with that drunken, no-good
pa of mine.

I haven't asked for much all these years
since I received Your Son, Jesus, as my Lord
and Savior. I know I don't have the right to
ask for more than You've already given me.
But I thought seeing as how it's been so many
years, and I haven't asked for anything up to
now, maybe You wouldn't mind doing me a
little favor. I was wondering if You could sorta
fix it so Luke decides to stick around these
parts. And just so You know, if it don't hap-
pen, I won't hold it against You.

Well, she'd done all she could. Now it was
up to Luke and God. She had work to do.

Luke paced the hallway outside of Pa's
bedroom door. Panic gripped him at the
groans of pain coming from beyond the
walls.

"I brought you some coffee."

He turned. His adopted sister, Emily, approached and handed him a steaming mug.

He took the cup gratefully and leaned
against the wall. Another moan escaped
through the walls. Luke's stomach knotted
even tighter, and he shook his head.

"You can't blame yourself, Luke." Emily's
own expression was filled with pain at the

sounds of agony coming from their pa's room.

"I should have insisted on getting rid of that old bull last year. It's almost like Ol' Angus knew he was about to be sold and wanted to punish Pa for it."

"Oh, Luke. Don't be silly. Ol' Angus just got through that fence at the wrong time, and Pa took the punishment for it. It was an accident. Just be glad you were there to take him down before he could kill Pa. God sent you along at the right time."

Luke sipped his coffee and studied Emily over the rim of the mug. Two years his junior, she could have passed for his twin with her carrot-orange hair, green eyes, and freckles. He couldn't count the times they'd been mistaken for blood relatives even though, in truth, Emily was Cassidy's niece. When her real pa had died of cholera, Cassidy had taken over Emily's care and had brought her along when she married Pa.

As though unaware of his scrutiny, Emily gave him a tender smile. "Really, you're a hero. Pa wouldn't be here at all now if not for you."

"I'm glad I was there, but it doesn't change the fact that I knew we needed to put in a new fence where Pa's crazy bull keeps getting out. Instead, I just patched it up again. If I had just gone with my gut, Pa wouldn't be laid out flat in there. What if Sam can't save his leg?"

Luke shuddered at the thought. What would Pa do if he lost his leg?

"We just have to pray hard," Emily replied firmly, reaching for him. Luke accepted the proffered hand and closed his eyes.

"Dear Lord," Emily prayed. "You see our pa in there, and You know how serious his condition is. We ask You to spare his life. That's the most important thing. Please give Sam wisdom and guide his hands. If possible, please help him to save Pa's leg. But if it's already too far gone, please give Pa the grace to accept it and to live with it. In Jesus' name, amen."

Luke pushed away the thought. He didn't want to consider the possibility that God wouldn't save Pa's leg. God could do a miracle. He'd done plenty, and Luke had even witnessed a few. Surely saving Pa's leg wasn't too much trouble.

"Why don't we go sit with Ma awhile?" Emily suggested. "She's pretty shaken up. Sam won't let her anywhere near the bedroom."

"It's just as well she can't hear Pa groan." Luke cast a glance at the closed door and headed into the sitting room.

Hours later, Sam emerged, pale and shaken.

"How is he?" Cassidy asked, her eyes wide with fright.

Sam sank to the nearest chair and jammed his fingers into his thick hair, raking back the black locks with one quick swipe. He leaned his elbows on his knees and regarded his family wearily. "I've never seen so many lacerations on one leg. I lost count of the stitches."

"You saved the leg, then?" Luke asked.

Sam's blue eyes filled, and his voice faltered. "I don't know. We have to keep the wounds clean and pray infection doesn't set in. To tell you the truth, even if Pa gets to keep his leg, there is no telling how much damage that bull did to the muscles. Pa may never have use of it again."

As though the burden of the past hours overwhelmed him, Sam buried his face in his palms and wept like a baby.

Cassidy stood immediately and went to him. She knelt on the wooden floor and took him into her arms. "Shh. You did all you could."

"What if it wasn't enough? Why did Doc Simpson have to be out of town now, of all times?"

"You are a capable doctor. Would your

father-in-law have done anything different than you did?"

"I don't think so. There wasn't much to do but stitch him up and pray for the best."

"All right, then," Cassidy said with a nod. "I remember Doc Simpson saying once that even doctors can't control what God ordains. You just have to do the best you can and leave the rest up to the Lord. Your pa knows that. No matter what happens, you have to believe God is in control. That way, you can't take the credit for the successes or the blame when things don't work out." She smiled and stood. "May I go to him?"

"I have him heavily medicated with chloroform," Sam replied, once again the professional doctor rather than the broken son. "Hopefully he'll sleep through the night. When he wakes up, the pain will be nearly unbearable."

"I'd still like to sit with him," Ma insisted.

Sam nodded. "Go ahead. But there'll be a lot of moaning in his sleep. Make sure you come out if it begins to bother you. Pa won't even know you're there, much less when you leave."

"Thank you, Sam. Emily made up your old bed for you. Go get some rest. I'll wake you when your pa rouses."

"Want me to ride over and tell Camilla

you'll be staying over tonight?" Luke asked, feeling suddenly as though he needed to do something . . . anything to feel useful.

"No need. She'll expect it." Sam stood. "I'm going to try to catch a few hours of sleep. Wake me if you need me."

"Thank you for everything, Sam. Try to cast the worry of this over on the Lord and get some rest," Ma said. "Good night."

"May I come with you and sit with Pa for a few minutes, Ma?" Emily asked softly, her voice trembling.

"Of course." Cassidy slipped her arm about Emily's shoulders, and they headed down the hall to the bedroom.

Luke watched as Sam followed, then turned at the bedroom they had once shared.

He released a heavy sigh and stoked the fire, watching the sparks fly upward. What if Pa never regained use of his leg again or lost it altogether? Then Luke would have no choice but to stay on indefinitely and run the ranch for the family. He would never get to Oregon. His mind rejected the thought instantly as guilt crept over him. How could he even think about himself at a time like this?

With a sigh, he added a log to the fire. After he was satisfied it would keep the house sufficiently warm until he returned, Luke slipped into his coat and wrapped a scarf around his neck. Feeling the heavy weight of responsibility on his shoulders, he stepped into the blustery November night to attend to chores and make sure all was well on the ranch.

CHAPTER 6

Laney waved hello to Emily and pulled Colby to a stop in front of the St. John ranch house. She leaned forward and rested her elbow on the saddle horn. Emily smiled a greeting and stooped over the scrub board, attempting to clean a pair of trousers.

"Morning," Laney said, noting that Emily's hands were red from the December cold. "Why are you washing out here on such a cold day?"

Emily shrugged and smiled. "Ma's getting caught up on the cleaning. I didn't want to be in the way."

"Where's Luke?"

Emily straightened and gave her a weary smile. She pressed her hands against her back and stretched.

"Down by the creek." She squinted and cupped her hand over her eyes to shield them against the sun's bright rays. "Haven't seen you around in a few days. You heard about Pa?"

Laney gave her a sober nod. "That's why I'm here. How's the leg looking today?"

It had been three days since Anthony had ridden out to the soddy to let them know about the accident, but Laney hadn't been able to bring herself to face the family. Guilt bit her deep. She had prayed for God to keep Luke in Kansas, so she figured her prayer was to blame for Papa Dell's condition.

Emily's shoulders rose and fell. "Not good. Sam's trying to put on a brave face, but you know how hard it is for him not to show his emotions. I'd say it's only a matter of time before he takes the leg." Her voice faltered. "Poor Sam. I can't imagine what he's going through."

And poor Luke. Laney knew Luke must be feeling torn between his responsibility to his family and grief over the loss of his dream.

"Do you want to come in and say hi to Pa? He'd probably welcome the distraction."

Laney just couldn't look Papa Dell in the eye, knowing she was responsible for the accident. "Maybe another time. I think I'll go find Luke."

"I think he just needed to get away from

the ranch and try to think straight. You know he'll have to postpone his plans to head west?"

"Yeah, I reckon he will." That was her fault, too. "I'll see you around, Em."

"All right. If you find him, tell him not to worry about evening chores. Will and Hope are pitching in to get them done."

"Hope?"

Emily grinned. "I promised her I'd bake an apple pie."

Laney shook her head and returned Emily's smile. "If that little sister of yours doesn't stop being ruled by her belly, she'll be as fat as Mr. Moody's prize sow."

"It's just baby fat," Emily replied, defending the chunky young girl. "She'll grow out of it."

"Probably." Laney glanced uncomfortably toward the direction of the river. She wanted to leave before Mama Cassidy discovered she was out here and insisted she go inside. "Well —"

"Sure you can't come in and say hi to Ma and Pa?"

"I'd better go find Luke. Tell Papa Dell I'm praying for him and that I'll be over soon to see him."

"Okay."

Laney could tell Emily was confused. But

for the moment, Laney's need to find Luke ruled her reluctance to hurt the young woman, dear as she was.

Laney turned her mount toward the river and rode off at a gallop. Her heart picked up a beat when she reached the river and spied Luke seated on the bank. He glanced up and waved as she dismounted and slipped Colby's reins around the branches of a nearby bush.

"What are you doing here?" he asked, his voice laced with sarcasm. "Rumor has it you're busy as ever, even with Granny's help — too busy to come to the ranch and see how Pa is."

It was true. She was busier than ever. The addition of ready-made dresses to Tucker's Mercantile had been such a success with the ladies of Harper, Tucker had offered her a 10 percent increase in her profits to take on more orders. Even with paying Granny a salary, she was coming out with more than before Granny moved in. If things continued as they were, the soddy would easily be paid off next spring — on time and in full. She couldn't help the thrill she felt as she watched her dream draw closer and closer to becoming a reality.

She chose to ignore Luke's comment about her not coming to the ranch to see

Papa Dell and focused instead on the business. "Will came by and drove Granny into town to drop off the gowns we finished this week and to pick up some more orders from Tucker." Laney dropped to the cool ground next to him and sent him a sideways grin. "Between you and me, I think Tucker and Granny are sweet on each other. I won't be surprised if there's another wedding in the family before long."

Luke grinned. "Wouldn't surprise me, either." The grin faded almost as quickly as it had appeared, and he leaned in closer. Laney shrank back at the intensity of his gaze. " 'Course, that's not the family wedding I had hoped to attend next."

"Oh, Luke. Please don't start a fight." Laney turned and stared out across the rippling water. "I came out to tell you how sorry I am about your pa."

"Are you?" He gave a short laugh and tossed a stick into the water. "Looks like things worked out just the way you wanted them to."

Laney's blood heated at the insinuation, but she knew Luke was spoiling for a fight as a way to relieve his frustration. She prayed for patience.

"You think I'd want you to stay here for my sake, at your pa's expense? You must not think very highly of me."

His brow furrowed in suspicion. "It never occurred to you that now I'd have to stay and run the ranch?"

"Of course it occurred to me. But not for the reason you suppose. I wouldn't marry you and be second choice to your dreams, anyway. Besides, maybe Sam will be able to save the leg, and you won't have to postpone your move after all. If that's all you care about." He was getting her riled again.

Luke's face darkened. "Even if Pa doesn't lose his leg, he'll probably never gain use of it again. If I don't run the ranch, who will?"

"I could." She'd thought of it before. It would mean sacrificing her herd for a while, but it seemed to be the least she could do after praying for something to happen to change Luke's mind about leaving. She'd rather run the ranch herself than to live with the guilt.

He studied her so intently, Laney felt warmth creep to her cheeks. "What about your soddy and the herd?"

She shrugged. "I almost have enough saved to pay off the soddy. I can wait until Will's old enough to take over the ranch before I build my own herd."

"You really think you could handle running the ranch?"

Was he thinking of letting her try?

"Why not? I've worked with you and Papa Dell long enough to know the ins and outs of St. John Ranch. I could probably run it in my sleep."

A sigh escaped from deep within Luke. "No, you couldn't. I have to be the one to stay — as usual."

Laney shot to her feet. She glared down at Luke, hands on her hips. "Luke St. John, you are acting like a —" Oh, what was he acting like? She stomped her foot on the ground. "You know how you're acting! And Papa Dell would probably rather sell off this place to the highest bidder than to let you run it with that attitude. He's up there in the house, about to have his leg chopped off, and listen to you — throwing sticks in the river and crying like a baby because you don't get to go west and build a bigger herd than your pa's."

"I am not crying!"

"You might as well be." She stomped to Colby and grabbed his reins from the bush. "I'm ashamed of you."

Luke felt his ears burn as he watched Laney ride away at breakneck speed.

Serves you right, he chided himself. Everything Laney said was true. Shame seared him. Not only had he insulted her by insinuating she was glad he had to stay in Kansas, he had made a fool of himself, complaining about running the ranch for his injured pa. What kind of man was he, anyway? This proved he didn't have half the backbone he'd always thought he had.

He knew Laney had been serious about putting her plans for her own land on hold so he didn't have to postpone heading west. She had more character than he did. Suddenly he knew he had to do what was right and stop complaining about it. God knew what was best.

Forgive me, Lord.

A heartfelt prayer. So powerful in its simplicity. Luke felt the change immediately and smiled. God had a way of changing a man with the smallest of adjustments.

And with that adjustment, Luke determined not to make any more plans to head west. Instead, his imagination headed in another direction: Laney. What if he married her and helped her start a herd for them next to his pa's ranch? Of course, they'd have to wait awhile to see what happened with Pa.

The sound of hooves pounding hard on the earth drew his attention back to the present. He glanced up to find Laney heading back. Luke grinned. She would love to hear that she'd actually won an argument, even if she hadn't stuck around to see him admit to being wrong.

His grin faded abruptly when he saw her pale face. She brought Colby to a skidding halt a few feet from where Luke stood.

He hurried to her and grabbed the horse's bridle. "What's wrong?"

"Get home, Luke. Your pa's leg's turned gangrenous. He's delirious from a high fever, and Sam is going to amputate. He needs your help."

"Oh, Luke, thank heaven you're here." Ma's tear-streaked face greeted him when he walked in the house moments later. "Sam needs you."

"What can I do?"

"Honey, you'll have to hold your pa's leg still while Sam amputates." Her voice broke. "I'm sorry, but Sam says it needs to come off immediately."

The blood drained from Luke's face. He felt the pressure of Laney's hand on his arm, but he couldn't respond.

Sam emerged from the bedroom. He gave Luke a cursory glance. "Good. You're here. Let's get it done before that poison spreads. Pa's fever shot up in a matter of minutes."

Luke swallowed hard and hung back. The pressure of Laney's hand on his arm increased. "Luke, you can do all things through Christ who strengthens you. Trust God to get you through this. But you have to go help. Sam needs you. Your pa needs you."

Her words shook him from his numbing state of dread. He covered her hand with his and squeezed. "Thank you, Laney. Pray for us."

Tears pooled in her eyes. "I am."

He gathered a shaky breath and followed Sam to their pa's room.

Laney prayed throughout the night. She prayed for Luke, for Sam, and most of all for Papa Dell. *Oh, God, he doesn't deserve this. I'm so sorry. I'll do anything if You'll just keep him alive.*

Finally Luke emerged, tears streaming down his face. Heedless of Mama Cassidy, Emily, and Tarah's presence, Laney jumped from her seat and went to him. He dropped to his knees and grabbed on to her, holding so tightly, it seemed he would crush her with his iron grip. She wrapped her arms about him and stroked his hair. Sobs shook his body, and Laney held him more tightly, her own tears flowing unchecked down her face.

They stayed wrapped in each other's arms until Sam appeared several minutes later. Laney withdrew first. Luke stood and grabbed his handkerchief from his pocket, then crossed the room. "I'll be back," he said to no one in particular. Laney let him go, sensing his need to be alone.

"How is your pa, Sam?" Cassidy's face showed the signs of her worry. She seemed older than Laney had ever noticed.

Sam pinched the bridge of his nose. His shoulders slumped. "The next few days will tell. We need to keep the wound clean, which means changing the bandages more often than I can be here to attend to it."

"Show me what to do next time they have to be changed, and I'll tend my husband."

Sam nodded and squeezed her hand. "His fever is extremely high. I'm going to pack ice around him to get it down. We still have a rough few hours ahead of us. Luke is hitching the wagon now to go into town and get some ice from the icehouse."

"Is Luke going to be all right?" Mama Cassidy asked. "He fell apart as soon as he came out of the room, but Laney was here to comfort him."

Embarrassed at the memory of Luke in

her arms right in front of the family, Laney shifted her gaze downward and studied the floor's wooden slats.

"He was a rock in there. I couldn't have done it without him. To tell you the truth, I was wishing for my wife's arms when I left that room. Sometimes no one can comfort us like the women we love. Luke will be all right. Don't worry."

The woman he loves. Does Luke still love me?

CHAPTER 7

Luke pushed his Stetson off his forehead, taking in the scene before him. He reveled in the beauty of the wide-open prairie blanketed in the first snowfall of the year.

Did Oregon smell this fresh and crisp in early winter?

Impatiently he pushed the thought aside, determined nothing would spoil the moment for him. He always looked forward to coming out to the south pasture and looking over St. John land at the first snowfall. The difference this year was that Pa wasn't with him as he always had been for the snow ride. Luke released a heavy sigh and turned Rusty back toward the house.

Three weeks had passed since Pa's operation. Two days after the surgery, his temperature returned to normal and he regained consciousness. His stump showed no signs of infection, and Sam was growing optimistic about his chances of recovery.

Sam said they could eventually order an artificial leg, and Pa should be able to lead a fairly normal life. Until then, the most important thing was that he gain strength. For now, even the briefest excursions from bed exhausted him.

Pa never complained . . . had even made a joke about having a funeral for the missing leg. But Luke knew the weakness had to be difficult for him.

Despite the tragedy of Pa's getting his leg amputated, Thanksgiving had held special meaning for the entire St. John family this year. "Thank You, Lord" seemed to be more heartfelt than ever before.

As Luke approached the ranch, he noticed a commotion and nudged Rusty to a trot. Disheveled and unshaven, Anthony sat in his wagon seat, his face drained of color.

"What's wrong?" Luke asked.

"Tarah's time has come. I brought the kids over for Emily to keep an eye on, and your ma is coming with me to the house."

"Sam know?"

"He knows, but as usual, Tarah refuses to allow him to deliver the baby. He's there just in case there's trouble, but she wants Granny and your ma. I'm headed over to Laney's next to get Granny."

"Want me to ride ahead and let her know

you're coming?"

"Would you? That'll save us some time."

Luke grinned as he rode off toward Laney's soddy. After a man had been with his
wife through the births of three children,
number four should be a matter of course.
But Anthony fell apart with each birth.

As Rusty made steady progress in the
newly fallen snow, Luke allowed his mind
to wander toward the future day when he
would have his own children. He continued
to daydream until Laney's soddy came into
view, then he rode with purpose.

Recognizing Luke's horse through the
window, Laney inwardly groaned. What was
he doing here at this time of day? And why
did Granny have to choose now to fix the
hem on little Sarah Jean Taylor's dress? It
was humiliating enough for Laney that a
ten-year-old's dress fit her, but Luke would
tease her unmercifully.

"Hold still," Granny scolded. "How will I
ever get this hem straight with your fidget-
ing?"

"Sorry, Granny. Luke's here."

"Well, whatever he wants will just have to
wait until I finish pinning this hem."

As if on cue, Luke tapped on the door.

"Come in, Luke," Granny called.

The door swung open. His gaze swept her, his eyes growing wide in surprise. He cleared his throat and averted his gaze. Heat burned Laney's cheeks. She knew what a spectacle she made, and she knew he was fighting to keep from laughing out loud at the sight of her.

He cleared his throat. "I'm sorry to interrupt, Granny."

"You should be. It's not as if we aren't working our fingers to the bone to get these gowns to Mr. Tucker. There's no time for constant interruptions."

"I know, Granny. And again, I'm sorry, but Anthony's on his way over with Ma. Tarah's time has come, and you know she won't have the baby without you."

"Now why didn't you say so? Help me up from here."

Luke strode across the room and took Granny's arm as she struggled to her feet. "The hem is pinned, Laney. You can sew it and deliver the dress to Tucker by tomorrow with the rest of the gowns, right? Mrs. Taylor has been hounding the poor man for a week about this dress."

Laney snorted and hopped off the chair. "Yes, we don't want Mrs. Taylor to pop her corset strings, worrying about her little girl's dress being ready in time for the Christmas dance."

"Don't be impertinent. I know you never liked the woman, but she's still your elder. And you shouldn't be discussing ladies' undergarments in front of Luke."

Amusement tipped the corners of Luke's lips. "I think you should make yourself a dress just like that one, Laney. It's nice to see you in girl clothes for a change — even little girl clothes."

The ruffly dress only reached Laney's midcalf. She straightened her shoulders, pretending she didn't care what he thought. "You know Sarah Jean is big for her age. Can I help it if she's as tall as I am?"

"No need to get riled. I think you look very sweet," he baited.

"Luke . . . ," Laney warned. "Will you get out of here so I can take off this ridiculous getup?"

"Too late." Luke chuckled and opened the door.

Laney heard the wagon rattle to a halt just as Luke spoke. She groaned aloud. Must everyone in the family see her dressed like a little girl?

Luckily Granny had a bundle ready and quickly headed toward the door. "Now don't you work yourself to death while I'm gone, you hear? I'll be staying with Tarah for a few days to help out."

Laney kissed the leathery cheek. "Don't worry, Granny. I'll be fine. Give Tarah my love, and tell her as soon as she's up to it, I'll be over to see her and the baby."

After the wagon rolled away, Laney braced herself for more teasing. Instead, Luke turned to her. "I'll go outside while you change, but I'd like to talk to you for a few minutes before you get back to work."

"Sure." Laney's stomach jumped at the seriousness of his tone. When the door was safely closed behind Luke, she hurriedly removed the dress and laid it across the table to be sewn. Then she slipped on her shirt and jeans and pulled on her boots. She only prayed Papa Dell hadn't taken a turn for the worse.

"Come on in, Luke," she called. "I'm decent."

He came back in and smiled, his gaze sweeping her. "Now that's my Laney."

Her stomach hopped at his tone. Was she his Laney?

"What did you want to tell me?"

Luke hesitated. "I don't know how you feel about this," he began, his voice shaky, words stilted.

"About what?"

"Well, just hang on. I'm trying to tell you."

Laney's defenses rose at his impatient tone. "Sor–ry! I don't got all day to wait on you, Luke St. John. You know I have a pile of work to do since Granny's going to be at Tarah's."

Slapping his Stetson against his thigh, Luke let out a growl. "Just forget it, Laney. I declare, a fella can't even propose to you without a big argument!"

He stomped off and mounted Rusty. He galloped away, leaving Laney to stare after him.

Propose? Excitement wiggled around in her stomach. If Luke was ready to propose again, he must have made the decision to stay and run the ranch for Papa Dell. She inwardly berated herself. If she didn't stop running him off, he might never marry her!

She tried to get back to work, but she couldn't help casting frequent glances toward the window, hoping Luke would come back. If he did, she would greet him at the door with a smile and be ready to throw herself into his arms if he decided to ask her to marry him again. She waited the rest of the morning, but hope gave way to despair when lunchtime arrived and he still hadn't returned.

After shrugging into her sheepskin coat,

Laney grabbed the water pail and made the short walk to the creek. She planned to dig a well come spring, but for now, the daily trip wasn't too awfully bad. It gave her a good excuse to escape the confines of the soddy and stretch her legs for a few minutes.

She squatted down beside the creek where the clear water rippled over a bed of rocks. Suddenly an eerie feeling slithered over her. The hairs on the back of her neck stood up. Laney hurriedly finished filling her pail and rose. Why hadn't she thought to buckle on her Colt? That would have made her feel a sight more comfortable right now.

Casting a wary glance over her shoulder, Laney picked up her pace, sloshing water from the pail. "Luke? Is that you? You're not scaring me, so you might as well show your face."

A twig snapped behind her, and Laney grinned and swung around. Expecting to startle Luke and get the upper hand, she stopped short and gasped as she came face-to-face with a tall man dressed in black. His brilliant blue eyes swept over her, and a smirk tipped the corners of sensual lips.

She willed her hands to stop trembling and made a mental note to get herself a big dog. "Who are you?" she demanded, her heart pounding like Indian drums during a rain dance. "And what are you doing on my land?"

He cocked an eyebrow. "Your land? Since when do they hand out property to children?"

Laney sneered. "I'm no child, mister. I'm a grown woman, and I own this patch of land your no-good carcass is standing on."

A slow smile slid across his face. "A woman, eh? Well, in that case . . ." He reached for her. Laney recoiled and drew back her arm, ready to strike if he dared to lay a hand on her.

"That's enough, Matt. No one said you could manhandle my daughter. Look at her. She ain't worth the bother, nohow."

Laney froze, fear causing the bile to rise in her throat. She'd know that voice anywhere. Slowly she turned. "Pa," she whispered. The sight of him shocked her. This man was a mere shadow of the pa she remembered.

"That's right. It's me. Looks like you done real good fer yerself, girlie."

"Wh–what do you want? You know there's a wanted poster up at Tucker's with your face plastered on it?"

"Then it's lucky fer me an' Matt here that I got me a girl with her own place."

Laney gave him a short laugh. "You don't

think you're staying with me?"

His face darkened. "You ain't changed a bit. Still as mouthy as ever." He brought his hand hard across her cheek. The ground came up to meet her, and she sprawled in the snow, tasting blood. He stood over her, intimidating even with sunken cheeks and bony arms.

She swiped at her mouth with the backs of her fingers and glared up at her pa. Her lips curled into a sneer. "You haven't changed either. Still enjoy bullying anyone smaller than you."

He moved closer, but Matt stepped between them. "Leave the girl alone. How's she going to go into town for supplies if she's all bruised up?"

Matt reached down. Ignoring his outstretched hand, Laney hopped to her feet. "What makes you think I won't go straight to the sheriff if you let me go into town?"

"I'll show you," Pa said, a coarse grin twisting his thin lips. He turned toward a nearby tree. "Get out here."

Laney watched in bewildered silence as a young girl of no more than five or six years stepped slowly into view. Even with her hair matted and her face covered in dirt, Laney could see the unmistakable resemblance to her own hair and features. This child was family.

Laney glowered at her pa. "Don't tell me you found another woman dumb enough to marry you."

Matt chuckled.

Her pa's eyes glittered dangerously. "I didn't marry her. But that didn't stop her from getting in a fix with this one." He jerked his thumb toward the little girl.

Laney ignored his crude comment and focused on the child. She smiled, trying to wrap her mind around the fact that now she had a little sister to look out for. Wait 'til Ben found out about this! For the first time, Laney was glad her brother had gone east to seminary. At least he would escape Pa's meanness this time around. "What's your name, honey?" she asked.

The little girl ducked her head.

Pa nudged her forward. "Yer big sister's talkin' to you, girl."

"Leave her be, Pa. She's just a little girl — not that showing kindness to children was ever your strong suit."

The little girl glanced shyly at Laney. Laney smiled at her and winked. Beautiful blue eyes grew wide, and she smiled back, revealing a missing front tooth.

"What's your name?" Laney asked again.

"Jane," she said in a barely audible voice. "The perfect name for a sister."

Jane's face lit up. Laney could well imagine how she felt. She knew from experience that one kind word from a stranger could make all the difference in a lonely child's life. Stepping toward her sister, Laney reached for her hand. "Are you hungry?"

Jane nodded.

"Well, let's go find you something to eat."

The little girl slipped a dirty hand inside Laney's, then to Laney's surprise, she turned and reached for Pa. He cleared his throat. "I'm coming."

Laney ignored the two men, though she knew they were following. Her mind raced. What was she going to do? Her Colt was hanging on a hook just inside the door. What if she could get inside first and grab it before Pa and his thug friend could stop her? She picked up her pace a bit, pulling Jane along with her. When she reached the soddy, she quickly pushed open the door. She stopped short and gasped. A man sat at her table, a cigar between his teeth.

Her gaze flew to the peg where the gun belt usually hung.

"Looking for this?" The man at the table held her Colt in his palm.

Laney shuddered in anger. Her pa was a

good-for-nothing varmint to bring these rascals to her house.

She heard a chuckle next to her ear and spun around, once again coming face-to-face with Matt. Laney shuddered at the clear message written in his dark eyes. She couldn't escape, so she might as well forget the idea. But he didn't know Laney Jenkins. She'd get out of this mess one way or another. They'd be sorry they ever tangled with her in the first place!

CHAPTER 8

"He's another good-looking baby, Tarah,"
Luke fibbed. Just a little fib — no use hurting his sister's feelings, even if the wrinkly,
squalling infant was slobbering all over the
front of his shirt.

Tarah took the baby and cuddled him
close, instantly halting Johnny's wails. A
laugh erupted from the four-time mother.
"Don't worry, Uncle Luke. He'll get better
looking every day." She kissed the top of
her baby's head and lowered herself into a
rocking chair next to the cozy fireplace.

Luke averted his gaze while his sister
prepared to nurse Johnny. When she was
settled and covered with a shawl, she said,
"Your first few days on this earth, I was so
embarrassed, I begged Ma and Pa not to
take you anywhere."

Luke sent her a sheepish grin. "I couldn't
fool you, eh?"

"Don't worry about it. I think he's just

beautiful. So how are things at the ranch?"

"Running smoothly."

"And Pa? How is he?"

"Stronger every day. Still a long ways from running a ranch, though."

"I'm sorry, Luke. I know it doesn't seem fair that you have to put your plans on hold."

A shrug lifted his shoulders. "You know, at first I was bitter about it. But after a good tongue lashing from someone near and dear to us both, I saw that I was just being selfish."

Tarah laughed. "Our Laney has a way of getting straight to the heart of the matter, doesn't she?"

He grinned. "I guess so."

"Speaking of Laney, I thought she'd have come to see Johnny by now."

"She hasn't been by?"

Tarah shook her head. "I suppose she's extra busy since Granny's staying with me, but I thought she'd have taken a few minutes to come meet the baby. You know how she loves to cuddle newborns."

Laney's adoration of infants was legendary in the family. Anthony good-naturedly said it was like trying to wrestle a piece of meat away from a grizzly to get to hold his own children when they were babies.

"Doesn't sound like Laney, does it?"

"Has anyone checked on her in the last few days?"

Luke shifted uncomfortably in his chair. "I don't guess so."

"She's probably working herself to death, with no one to make sure she's eating and sleeping properly. Could you run by there after you get Ma's supplies from Tucker's?" She stopped short and stared at him. A frown furrowed her brow. "What?"

"What, what?"

"You're staring at your boots. What's wrong?"

"Laney and I got into it last time I saw her. I doubt she'd want to see me."

Shaking her head, Tarah huffed. "Honestly. You two beat all I ever saw and then some. You're either kissing or arguing."

"Who's kissing?" Little D entered the room, trailing mud. "Uncle Luke and Laney? Yuck. Not again."

"Little D! Look at the floor. Granny just scrubbed it yesterday. She'll tan your hide for this." Tarah gave him a stern look. "Take off those boots, and go get a bucket of water. You can just clean it up before she sees it."

Little D looked scandalized. "You want me to do women's work?"

Luke bit back a grin and stood as Tarah's eyes narrowed. The boy was about to get a stern lecture, and Luke didn't want to be around to witness it.

Obviously Little D caught the look, too, for he scooted off to fetch the water.

Tarah's glance swept upward until her gaze caught Luke's. "Will you go by Laney's? She's probably forgotten all about your argument. Besides, I'm a little worried about her."

Luke grabbed his hat from the table and headed for the door. "All right. I'll swing by there after I pick up Ma's supplies from Tucker's."

A relieved smile crossed Tarah's lips. "Thank you."

Luke bid her good day and stepped outside. The sun, beating brilliantly against the snow, nearly blinded him, and he squinted against the brightness. He climbed into the wagon and made his way to Tucker's.

Tucker glanced up and grinned as the bell above the door announced Luke's entrance into the dusty mercantile.

"Howdy, there, Luke. How's that pa of yers doin'?"

Luke's spine stiffened. It was one thing to give family news to other family members like Tarah, another entirely to give the townsfolk more to gossip about. Nevertheless, he attempted a cheery response. "He's gaining strength every day."

"Glad to hear it," Tucker said, nodding. "I hated to hear about such a fine man losing a leg, but I guess the good Lord knows whut He's a-doin'."

"He always does," Luke replied, handing Tucker his list. "Ma sent me in for these."

"I'll git right on it." He scanned the list, then turned and pulled a large sack of flour from the shelf behind him. "I hear the reverend and Tarah got another blessin' t'other night."

"Yep. Another boy to keep Tarah on her toes."

"Not much of a looker, from what yer granny says. 'Course, I ain't likely one to judge, bein' as I ain't never had one of my own."

Luke grinned. "Tarah says they all look like that in the beginning, but she's convinced he'll handsome right up with time."

"I'm sure that'll be a relief."

Tucker continued to fill the order for Cassidy, then he paused and squinted at Luke. "You seen Laney, by any chance?"

Why did everyone seem to think he should be keeping up with Laney? Irritation taunted Luke, daring him to spout off to the old man, but he bit back a retort, determined not to offend. "I haven't seen her in a few days."

Tucker shook his head, his brow furrowed. "That's right peculiar."

"What is?"

A shrug lifted his shoulders. "She came in for supplies yesterday, but she didn't bring the gowns she owes me. Nearly bit off my head fer asking about 'em. Then I seen her duck into the saloon."

"The saloon? Laney hates the sight of that place."

"That's whut I thought, too. That's why it struck me as peculiar to see her go in there." The storekeeper leaned across the counter and lowered his voice. "You don't think she's been working so hard it finally got to her, do you?"

A frown creased Luke's brow. "What are you saying?"

"Think Laney coulda took to the drink like her pa?"

"Laney?" Luke laughed at the thought.

"Been known to happen." He shoved his finger toward Luke. "It's a sorry enough sight to see a man all liquored up, but a drunken woman is downright shameful."

Still grinning, Luke paid Tucker and grabbed the crate. "You don't have to worry about Laney turning to the drink. For one thing, she hates it because of her pa; for another, she's a Christian. She wouldn't do it because she believes it's wrong."

"Then what was she doin' sneakin' into the saloon?"

That was a puzzle. "I'm not sure, but let's give her the benefit of the doubt, okay? And I'd sure appreciate if you didn't mention it to anyone else."

Tucker's face darkened. "What do you take me fer, some gossipin' woman?"

Luke hid his amusement and turned. His eye caught the WANTED poster on the wall, and his mouth went dry. What if . . . ?

"I have to be going now, Mr. Tucker. Remember, don't mention Laney to anyone else."

Mr. Tucker's indignant response was lost on Luke's ears as he hurried from the mercantile, set the crate in the back of the wagon, and quickly climbed into the seat.

One thing was for certain. If her pa was back, Laney was in trouble. Luke's jaw clenched. But not as much trouble as the old man would be in if he laid one hand on her. Remembering that there were two men on the WANTED poster with Jenkins, Luke decided to stop off at the sheriff's office.

Sheriff Boggs, a middle-aged bachelor with graying temples, greeted Luke cordially. "What can I do for you, Luke?"

"I think Jenkins and his gang might be holding Laney out at her place." No point wasting time with small talk when Laney might be in trouble.

The sheriff's gaze narrowed, and he leaned forward with interest. "You saw them?"

"No, but Tucker noticed Laney headed into the saloon yesterday."

"Well, if she was in town, they aren't likely holding her." Sheriff Boggs scowled and tipped his chair back to rest on two legs.

"Unless they sent her to town for supplies — including liquor."

"That's an awful lot of supposin'. If I jumped to conclusions every time someone went into the saloon . . ."

"This is *Laney.* She'd never take a drink."

"I can't go rushing off to her place just because you don't like that she went into the saloon."

Luke wanted to grab the apathetic sheriff by the collar and send him across the room; instead, he reined in his anger and tried to reason with the poor excuse for a lawman. "Tucker said she snapped at him yesterday, and Tarah says she hasn't even been by to see the new baby yet."

Emitting a short laugh, the sheriff stood. "Listen, Luke. Laney Jenkins is as snarly as a bear most of the time, and if she hasn't been by to see your sister's new young'un, it's probably because she's busy sewing for Tucker."

Luke searched for something else to convince the sheriff. The man had a point on all accounts. Those things didn't necessarily mean Laney was in trouble, but Luke knew she was. He could feel it. And he hated to walk into a situation outgunned.

"Look, Sheriff, I'd be obliged if you'd just trust me and ride out there with me. Maybe I'm wrong, and if I am, Laney'll give me an earful; but if I'm right, we'll have saved her, and you'll have captured three outlaws."

The sheriff seemed to consider the idea for a moment and appeared as though he might give in when the door flew open.

"Sheriff, come quick. There's trouble down at the saloon. Some fella's been caught cheatin' at cards, and it looks like they're about to shoot him."

Sheriff Boggs grabbed his rifle from the wall and shrugged at Luke as he walked past him to join the messenger. "Sorry. I'll ride out there with you later, but I have to go put a stop to this before someone ends up dead."

Expelling a frustrated breath, Luke watched him go. Laney could just as easily be in trouble. He drove past Sam's office and stopped just as a man hurried inside carrying a small boy. The child appeared to have broken his arm. Sam would be busy for quite some time.

Determined not to waste another second, Luke said a hasty prayer and turned the horses toward Laney's soddy.

Laney jumped and glanced up from her sewing as a plate sailed across the room and hit the wall, flinging its contents all over the floor.

"This ain't fit to eat. How come you ain't never learnt to cook?"

Laney glowered at the unkempt cowboy called Abe. "Who taught you manners? At least I tried to cook a decent meal!"

"There ain't nothin' decent about that mess you tried to pass off as venison stew. That was just a waste of meat and vegetables."

"No one said you had to eat it!" Laney retorted.

"You best watch your sass, little girl, or I'll make you wish you'd been nicer. Now get yourself up and cook something we can eat."

"Cook it yourself," she shot back, returning her attention to her sewing.

Abe sprang from his chair and towered over her, his breath fouling the few inches of space between them. He grabbed her arm in a flash of movement, his fingers biting cruelly into her soft flesh.

Determined not to show the fear creeping into her belly, Laney met his gaze evenly. Sneaking vinegar into the stew had made her feel better, but maybe it hadn't been such a good idea after all. Of course, she'd dipped a little out for Jane and herself first, but Abe didn't have to know that.

"Leave her alone," Pa growled from a pallet next to the fire. "Can't you see she's busy?"

Obviously as surprised as Laney, Abe released her arm and turned to Jenkins. "Have you tried to eat the mess she's passin' off as grub? My dog wouldn't eat that slop."

"Then fix yer own grub and leave the girl be."

Her pa erupted in a deep cough, and for several minutes no one spoke while he hacked. Laney frowned. He had been coughing like this since he arrived. She tried not to care, but she couldn't help herself. He spent the majority of his time stretched out on a thin pallet in front of the stove.

When he rose, he trembled with weakness.

"I'm goin' out to try to find a rabbit to roast." Abe glared at Laney and yanked open the door, letting in a blast of cold air. "And don't think yer gettin' a bite of it!"

"I wouldn't take food from you anyway."

"What's wrong with you, Pa?" Laney asked after Abe slammed the door.

"Worried about your old pa, are ya, girlie? Must be gettin' soft. The girl I left would've been countin' the days 'til I keeled over."

"Forget I asked." Laney gave a short, bitter laugh. "And you didn't leave a girl behind. You sold me to the highest bidder like I was a slave. And Ben, too. You do remember Ben, don't you? Or have you forgotten about your son?"

"I ain't forgettin' him. I just figured he must be dead since you didn't mention him."

Laney fought to keep her temper in check. "I didn't mention him because you didn't ask. But I guess that's to be expected of someone like you."

His eyes narrowed, and his expression darkened. "Well, where is he, then? He couldn't be farmin' or ranchin' around here with that bum leg of his."

"Not that it's any of your business, but he happens to be back east, married to a pretty wife. He just finished seminary and was offered a church somewhere in Virginia."

"You mean to tell me my son's a preacher? A no-good, thievin' preacher?"

A coughing fit seized him as it did when he got too excited.

When he calmed, Laney met his gaze. "Ben's a preacher, but he's not a thief. Besides, you calling anyone a thief is sorta like the pot calling the kettle black, wouldn't you say?"

Jenkins shook his head in disgust. "I shoulda known better than to give you to that teacher and her preacher beau." He raised his brow in question. "I reckon they got hitched?"

"That's right. Tarah and Anthony took us in and raised us." She gave him a pointed look. "And you didn't *give* us away. You sold us."

"You don't have to keep reminding me of that, Laney-girl. I remember it like it were yesterday. So just shut up about it before I whale the daylights out of you."

Laney blinked in surprise. Not only was this the first time he'd used her name since he'd returned to her life, he seemed bothered by the memory of what he'd done. The thought raised her ire. She didn't want him to suddenly grow a conscience about it. If he cared, she might not be able to hate him, and he deserved her hatred — every bitter ounce that she'd harbored for as long as she could remember, and even more so since the day he'd taken ten dollars and a horse, then walked out of her life.

She wanted him gone. Out of her life again. "What do you plan to do, Pa? You know you can't hide out here forever."

He nodded. "Matt has plans for the bank in town. After that, we'll leave."

"You're going to rob the bank? Are you crazy? You can't do that." A gasp escaped Laney's lips. "My money is in that bank!" Her dreams for the future. "I'll lose my soddy and my land without that money."

His gaze searched hers. "I know you worked hard trying to buy this property. Don't know why you'd want it, but I know what it's like to lose. Wish it could be different, but Matt has his mind set on the bank. We need more money, iffen we're to get fer enough away that the law can't find us. After we do a number on the bank, we can split up."

"What makes you think I won't warn the sheriff next time you send me in for supplies and whiskey?"

He gave a short laugh. "You think I'd have told you if we was goin' to be around long enough? Matt's in town checkin' the layout of the place, and we're leavin' out tonight. 'Course, we'll have to tie you up when we go so's you don't go running to the law or those St. Johns. But I figure you'll get yourself loose pretty fast. From what I can tell, yer one smart girl."

"What about Jane?" Laney asked, ignoring the compliment.

"She ain't yer affair."

"She is, too. She's my sister!"

"You want her?"

"What's your price?" Laney curled her lip.

His face grew red, though from embarrassment or anger Laney wasn't sure. Nor did she have a chance to find out, as a coughing fit seized him.

"You shouldn't go out in this weather. What if you have pneumonia?"

"Don't tell me what to do, girl. Ain't no woman yet got by with orderin' me around, and I ain't starting with the likes of you."

"Fine. Catch your death, then. See if I care. What about Jane?"

"You can have her."

Laney hesitated, waiting for him to go back on his word. When he didn't speak, she finally broke the silence herself. "You mean it?"

He shrugged. "Like ya said, I'll probably

be dead sooner than later, and ain't no sense takin' the girl when she'll most likely have to fend for herself 'fore long."

Laney caught his gaze, searching for a trace of deception in his dark eyes. He stared back frankly, and when he looked away, Laney had the uncomfortable feeling it was from shame. Again, anger seized her at the compassion seeping in despite her determination to hold a grudge.

I don't want to feel sorry for him, Lord. He doesn't deserve it. Don't make me feel sorry for this worthless excuse for a man.

She glanced to the bed where Jane napped, one strawberry blond braid slung across her face. Laney's heart swelled with love. This little girl was her own flesh and blood. Laney smiled. Her sister would have roots here in Harper. She'd never feel like she didn't belong. She would grow up with Little D and the rest of Tarah and Anthony's children. Most of all, she would know her sister loved and wanted her.

Glancing at her pa, she couldn't help but notice he shivered, despite his close proximity to the fire. His back was turned, and even through the thin blanket, Laney could see his bones poking through. He wasn't long for this earth. A thought seized her. If her pa died, he wouldn't go to heaven. Her stomach quivered.

"Pa?"

"What?" he growled.

"Don't die without knowing Jesus."

"Shut up, girl, before I shut you up. You know I don't have no use for religion and such." He coughed. "Leave me alone and let me rest."

"Fine. I tried."

Laney turned back to her sewing.

Please send help, Lord. It's been four days, and no one has even come to check on me. Don't they notice I haven't been around? If I lose my money, I won't have a home for Jane. I can't bear the thought of her growing up without a sense of belonging like I did. Please, Lord. After what You did to Papa Dell, I've learned my lesson. I'm not asking for myself; I'm asking for Jane.

CHAPTER 9

Luke crept stealthily alongside the soddy until he drew near the window. Pressing his back against the outside wall, he craned his neck and peeked sideways through the window. Relief flooded him at the sight of Laney working diligently as though there wasn't an unkempt outlaw glaring at her from across the table. She glanced up and sneered at the dirty buckskin-clad man who tore off a bite of roasted meat, then licked his fingers.

Across the room, a man lay on a pallet close to the woodstove, and a small girl sat quietly on the bed, her gaze fixed on Laney. Luke studied the rest of the room. There were only two men. He couldn't move in until the third man showed up. Otherwise, the missing outlaw might come in at the wrong time and overpower Luke. Then he'd be no help for Laney.

Luke retreated slowly until he found a safe

place away from the soddy where he could watch without being discovered. He lay flat on his stomach. Snow soaked into his shirt and the front of his trousers, adding irritation to his anxiety.

Although he hated the thought of Laney staying in the soddy much longer, he couldn't help but feel a bit of relief that she appeared unmolested. Still, he'd feel a lot better when the other outlaw showed up. Once he did, Luke knew he could move in and get her out of there. A thought occurred to him. *What if the three men split up and the third outlaw isn't with them anymore?* Luke groaned inwardly. Laney might be in there with those men for nothing. *Show me what to do, Lord. I don't want to put Laney in danger.*

It seemed like an eternity of waiting without an answer from heaven. After two hours, Luke made up his mind. He was moving in. He started toward the soddy. A twig snapped behind him. Luke spun around, expecting to find the third outlaw poised to jump him. Instead, the sheriff stood before him, his six-shooter cocked and pointed.

"What are you doing here, Sheriff?" Luke whispered.

"You were right. The outlaws are holed up

at Laney's."

"What changed your mind?"

"I arrested one of them in the saloon today." The sheriff chuckled. "Not very smart for a wanted man to cheat at cards, if you ask me. Have you checked out the soddy?"

Luke nodded. "There are two men — although one of them appears to be sick. That one must be Jenkins. I recognized the other man from the poster. He's the only one with a gun. Besides those two, there's a little girl and Laney."

"All right, then," the sheriff said. "You go to the window and be ready to fire if necessary. I'll bust the door open and try to gain the upper hand without getting those two females hurt."

Soon they were in place. The second outlaw sat with his legs stretched out, his hat down over his face. His chest rose and fell evenly as though he slept. Suddenly the door burst open and the sheriff appeared, his rifle in one hand and a pistol in the other. The younger man started awake and nearly fell out of his chair as he recognized that he'd been caught. He stood and reached into the air. Laney grabbed his guns.

Luke moved around the soddy and entered.

Laney glanced up and gave him a cursory smile, then she turned back to the sheriff. "That's my pa over there, Sheriff," she said. "He's pretty sick."

"We'll get Sam over to take a look at him once I get him all locked up in the jail."

"Just get him out of my house, please." Her voice trembled slightly, and she passed her hand wearily across her forehead.

Luke strode across the room until he stood next to Laney. "Are you all right?"

She gave a nonchalant wave. "Oh, I'm fine. But they put me even further behind with Tucker. Think Granny's about ready to come back?"

Luke knew she was shaken and trying not to show it. Tenderness rushed through him. He brushed his thumb down her cheek, testing its softness. "I'm sure she'll be ready soon." He wanted to take her into his arms to reassure himself that she was truly all right, but he knew she'd balk at the gesture in front of anyone.

"Well, I suppose I'll get these two where they belong." The sheriff eyed Jenkins critically. "You don't look much like the man you used to be, Jenkins. I guess this is what hard living does to a man."

"Save your sermon, Sheriff," the bone-thin man replied with a sneer. "Just do what you gotta do."

"Can you sit a horse?"

"I'll hitch Laney's wagon and drive him into town," Luke volunteered. He'd left his own wagon a mile from the soddy to enable him to approach silently.

"No need for that," Jenkins growled. "I can sit a horse just fine." His last words were followed by an onslaught of coughing from deep within his chest.

Laney snorted. "Hitch the wagon, Luke. He couldn't ride ten feet without falling off."

Sheriff Boggs shoved the other outlaw out the door. "I'm taking this varmint on ahead. You follow as soon as you get the wagon hitched, will you, Luke?"

"Sure, Sheriff. We won't be long."

"What makes you think I won't make a run fer it?" Jenkins said, his voice trembling from his last coughing fit.

"You couldn't make it to the outhouse, let alone run away, Pa."

"You better just watch yourself. I can still tan your hide."

Laney snorted again, but the sheriff interrupted before she could reply. "We'll be going now."

"Might as well sit and wait," Jenkins grumbled, obviously too sick to keep up his grisly facade.

Once the door was closed behind the sheriff, Luke turned to Laney. "Why don't you pack a few things and ride along?" he suggested. "I'll drop you off at Anthony and Tarah's for the night so you don't have to stay alone."

"I told you, I have work to do. Besides, I won't be alone. Will I, Jane?"

Luke shifted his attention to the little girl on the bed. He'd forgotten she was even there. "Who's this?" he asked, smiling at the child. She ducked her head and trembled.

"I'm sorry," he said. "I didn't mean to scare her."

"It's all right," Laney said softly. She walked to the bed and pulled the girl in her arms. "This is my sister. I guess she'll be staying with me from here on out."

Luke raised his brow, trying not to show his shock at the news. He eyed the little girl and smiled. "It's nice to meet you," Luke offered. "I'm Luke, a good friend of your sister's. I hope we'll be friends, too."

Jane glanced at him, eyes wide, but she didn't speak, nor did she smile.

Luke cleared his throat. "I suppose I

should get that wagon hitched."

Laney watched Luke go, not sure what to say to her pa now that he was headed to jail. She turned and observed him wrapped in his blanket at the table.

White-hot anger burned inside of her. She wanted to be glad he was going to get what he deserved, but her anger warred with the compassion rising inside of her. He could be sentenced to hang, and if he did, he would die a sinner. He wouldn't last a week in prison.

God, what can I do about it? I already tried to share with him about Jesus, and he won't listen.

"Stop starin' at me like that, girl. I ain't no charity case."

Laney laughed at the ludicrous statement. "As long as I can remember, we lived on folks' charity, Pa. When did you suddenly grow a sense of pride?"

Jenkins glowered at her. "Maybe I wanted to make life easier for her," he said, jerking his thumb toward Jane.

"So making her travel with an outlaw gang and threatening to hurt her if I didn't co-operate was your way of making things easier? That doesn't seem too likely, Pa."

"I was just blowin' smoke. I ain't never

hit her even once, and I never would."

A bitter laugh erupted from Laney's lips. "First thing you did was knock me to the ground. Just like old times." Impatiently she pushed aside the hurt trying to shove its way in through the memories she'd tried to forget. What did she care if her pa loved her little sister but had never loved her?

He grimaced. "I know how stubborn you are. How was I supposed to keep ya in line without some sorta hold over ya? If I didn't remind ya who was boss and threaten to beat your sister, ya never would have obeyed. Then I couldn't have protected you from Matt and Abe, no matter how much rough talkin' I did."

Choosing to ignore the implication that he cared anything at all about her, Laney stepped closer and lowered her voice so Jane couldn't hear. "If you care so much about Jane, why didn't you take good care of her, Pa?"

His features darkened. "There was supposed to be enough money in that old fool's safe to make all three of us rich," he growled. "I was gonna buy us a little house somewhere where Janey could go to school like other little girls. I wanted her to be proud."

He began to cough again before Laney

could reply. She regarded him silently. Could he possibly be telling the truth? She recalled the last few days. He had protected both her virtue and well-being against Matt and Abe numerous times. She had to admit Jane wasn't afraid of him in the same manner she and Ben had been as children. And he seemed almost gentle when dealing with the little girl.

While Laney pondered these last thoughts, Luke returned. The door opened, letting in a blast of cold air and a swirl of snow.

"It's snowing again? Honestly, Luke. My pa will catch his death if he goes out in this."

Luke shrugged. "I don't see as how we have a choice in the matter."

"Go tell the sheriff we'll bring him in tomorrow if the snow has quit falling. No sense in having him keel over before the circuit judge comes through."

Laney noted the hesitation in Luke's eyes. His concern warmed her, and her lips tilted upward in a small smile. "Don't worry, Lukey. I'll be fine. Pa couldn't hurt a puppy in his condition."

"I suppose you're right. I'll run to town and talk it over with the sheriff, but if he objects, I may have to come back and get your pa."

Relief washed over her. "Thank you. I appreciate it."

"Can you walk me out?" he asked, lifting her coat from its peg next to the door. The intensity of his gaze sent a rush of warmth through Laney. He held her coat while she slipped her arms in it. Laney could feel the insistent pressure of his hands on her shoulders, and another wave of warmth covered her.

Laney turned to Jane. "Help Pa to his pallet, honey. I'll be right back."

Jane scooted off the bed and shuffled to Jenkins's side. "Come on, Pa," she said quietly. "Laney says you ain't gotta go nowheres tonight."

Laney's heart ached as she watched her pa smile at the child. In the first twelve years of her life, he had never once looked at her that way. She welcomed the frigid air as she stepped into the night. Luke snatched up her hand and tucked it through his arm.

"I'm going to ask Sam to come and take a look at Jenkins," Luke said. "So don't bring him in too early tomorrow. Wait for Sam."

"The sheriff said he'd have Sam take a look at him at the jail." Standing so close to Luke, Laney had difficulty concentrating.

"Your pa seems pretty bad off. If Sam suggests it, the sheriff might let him stay with you until the judge comes. You know as well as I do that could be anywhere from a week to two months, depending on where he is and how much crime there's been in the county."

Laney cringed inwardly at the very thought. Judges sometimes took months to respond to a summons. She didn't want Pa staying with her for days or weeks or months. Why shouldn't he be locked up like Matt and Abe? It was one thing to keep him overnight while it snowed, but two months? How would she ever put up with him that long? Why should she have to? He had sold away his rights to her eight years ago.

"Well?" Luke's voice broke through her bitter thoughts.

Laney shrugged. "I guess we'll wait and see what Sam thinks."

"What do you think?" he insisted. "If you don't want him here, I'll take him right now. It's your decision."

Laney tilted her head and regarded him frankly. "He'll stay the night, and after that, I just don't know."

They reached the wagon. Luke released her to pull the team back into the sod barn. Laney followed and helped him unhitch the horses.

When they finished, Luke leaned against the wagon and faced her. He captured both of her hands in his. "Are you all right?" he asked, his voice shaky with emotion. "They didn't hurt you?"

Laney smiled and shook her head. "They didn't lay a finger on me. Pa wouldn't let them, actually."

Relief washed over his features. He drew her close. Laney went willingly into his arms and nestled against his broad chest. She felt his hand stroke her hair. A sigh escaped her lips, and for the first time in days, the tension left her shoulders. "Thank you for coming for me, Luke."

Luke pulled slightly away and tipped Laney's chin upward until she met his gaze. "I'm sorry I let my pride keep me away as long as I did. I could have spared you sooner if I had come by to check on you."

Reaching up, Laney pressed her palm against his rough cheek. "None of this is your fault," she said softly, swallowing hard as she recalled the last thing Luke had said to her that day. He had wanted to propose. "I wasn't exactly nice to you last time we spoke."

"We do seem to bring out the temper in each other." Luke grinned and covered her hand with his. "But I'd rather be mad every day of my life and have you with me than live in peace with anyone else."

What exactly was he trying to say?

"Marry me, Laney."

She glanced at him cautiously. "Where have I heard that before?"

He sent her a heart-stopping grin. "I'll keep asking until I get you in front of a preacher, Laney Jenkins." He slipped his hands around her waist and pulled her close. "You're the only woman for me."

Laney's knees felt watery, and her senses reeled at the proximity of the man she loved. She swayed forward as his head slowly began to descend. Then, although it required every ounce of her will, she pressed her palm against his chest to deter him. "Wh–what about Oregon? I still can't move off away from here — especially now that I have my little sister to raise."

"I've decided not to go." Luke's eyes momentarily seemed to cloud in the soft glow of the lantern light.

"Why would you decide something like that?"

"Pa won't be up to sitting a horse again for quite a while, if ever. He needs me to run things for him. We might have to put off building our herd for a few years while I keep his operating until Will can take over. That okay with you?"

"Of course it is, Luke. I'll continue sewing for Tucker, and we can keep saving money." Laney's excitement grew with each word. "By the time we're ready, we'll have enough to buy a right fine herd to start us off."

A grin split Luke's face. "Are you saying yes, then?"

Laney's cheeks heated. "Of course my answer is yes!" She flung her arms around his neck and giggled when he lifted her off the ground.

He set her down and kept a steadying hand on her arm, allowing them both to regain their composure a moment before he pulled her close. "Thank you, Laney. I promise you'll never regret becoming my wife."

"I know I won't," she murmured just as his lips moved slowly over hers, drowning her words and pushing aside the doubts creeping into her mind.

Later, while she lay in the darkness next to Jane, listening to her pa's loud snoring, Laney recalled the faraway look in Luke's eyes when he told her he'd decided to stay in Harper and run St. John Ranch.

Unease gnawed at her. She had said she would never be second choice to Luke's dream. Would she ever believe he was stay-ing because he wanted to run the ranch and marry her, or would this anxiety always creep in during times of uncertainty? She tried to push the worry away. After all, she was getting everything she wanted — her own place, a means of making and saving money, her own herd eventually, and now the most important dream of all . . . she would soon marry Luke. So why was her stomach twisted in knots?

Closing her eyes, she tried to pray, but the words wouldn't come. Finally, after hours of trying not to toss and turn, she got up and stoked the fire to make sure Pa stayed warm, then she pulled out her sewing and went to work. Things were changing so fast, she was having trouble wrapping her mind around the reality of it all.

As she tried to sort it all out, her thoughts wandered away from the task at hand. She pricked her finger with a pin, and sudden tears sprang to her eyes. Then, as though she had opened a floodgate, the tears continued in a steady stream down her cheeks until the sobs wrenched her body.

Lord, I have everything I have ever dreamed of, and still I feel like there's a hole dug in my heart. What's wrong with me?

She felt a soft hand slip inside hers and looked up. Jane's brilliant blue eyes were flooded with tears, and she leaned her head against Laney's shoulder. "I been crying, too," she whispered. "I think Pa's real sick. Is that why you're crying, Laney?"

Laney held Jane more tightly, taking comfort from her warm little body as she pulled her onto her lap. "Partly, honey."

She stared at the child and wondered at her ability to love their pa. Maybe if he had treated Laney and Ben with an ounce of the affection he seemed to feel for Jane, she would be able to feel something for him, too. As it was, she was willing to let him stay until the judge came through — for Jane's sake, if nothing else. But once he was sentenced to his fate, she was through with him. For good.

CHAPTER 10

A persistent knocking at the door awakened Laney after barely two hours of slumber. Pa's coughing was getting worse, and sleep was sporadic, at best. The knock came again as she pushed back the quilts and swung her legs over the side of the bed. Turning, she replaced the covers over Jane.

"I'm coming," she called, her voice husky from sleep and irritation.

She grabbed her dressing gown and padded across the sod floor strewn with rag rugs. She lifted the latch and swung open the door.

"I declare. Who stays in bed two hours after sunup? Where is your sense of propriety, gal?"

"Granny! What are you doing here?" Glancing past her, Laney spied Anthony grinning broadly as he lifted his hand in farewell and flipped the reins at the horses.

"Humph." Granny walked right in,

thumping her cane against the floor. "I live here, remember — or have you thrown me out since I've been helping Tarah with her new baby?"

Laney felt her cheeks grow warm. "Of course I didn't throw you out. It's just that . . ."

Granny waved toward Jenkins's pallet. "Oh, him. Well, I know all about that rascal."

"My pa ain't no rascal!"

Laney started at Jane's outburst.

Granny cackled. "Heard about her, too. 'Course, I heard she was quiet as a mouse and not a thing like you. Maybe she's more like you than Luke gave her credit for."

"Maybe." The thought didn't entirely displease Laney. A woman needed a voice in this world.

Making her way to the bed, Granny eyed Jane sternly. "Now look here, I am your granny now, so you must watch how you speak to me. Is that understood?"

Jane trembled beneath the covers. Laney only prayed she didn't wet the bed from fear.

"Speak up. You weren't afraid to voice your opinion a minute ago."

"Yes, ma'am," Jane squeaked out.

"That's fine." Granny's stern face lit, and

she smiled. "Now I showed some mighty poor manners by calling your pa a rascal right in front of you. But I'll forgive you for sassing if you'll forgive me for my bad manners. How's that?"

Jane gave her a shy smile. "That's just fine, ma'am."

"I thought you looked like a girl with some good sense. Now you must call me Granny."

"Yes, Granny."

Laney stared in wonder at the exchange. Granny was a crotchety old woman, but she never ceased to amaze her.

"Get yourself dressed, Laney-girl. I'll put some coffee on to boil and start breakfast."

"But, Granny, you can't . . . well, I don't see how you can stay here. My pa has some sort of lung sickness. When Sam came by yesterday and examined him, he said we'd best keep him away from folks just in case it's contagious."

"Hogwash. I've nursed my share of disease-riddled men. I haven't taken even one man's sickness, and I don't figure to start at this late date."

Laney cleared her throat. "That's not the only reason. You might have noticed . . ."

"Oh, stop trying to be polite. Of course you don't have room for me to sleep here.

Anthony will be back to pick me up this evening after supper. In the meantime, I hear you're behind on your sewing for Mr. Tucker. I'm here to help."

"I don't know what to say."

"Don't say anything. Just go get dressed, and make the bed so we can get our day started. Now, Jane, I have a couple of sourballs and a book in my bag. After breakfast, if you'll sit quietly and look at your book, I'll let you have one sourball. How's that sound?"

"Just fine, Granny. Just fine!"

For the next two weeks, Granny came every day but Sunday. Laney's nest egg continued to grow, and she looked excitedly to the day she could slap down a large last payment and get the deed to her property.

So far no one had said a thing about the engagement — neither Granny, nor Mama Cassidy at church, nor Tarah. Obviously Luke hadn't mentioned his proposal to anyone. Laney felt a little disappointed. Her growing pessimism over Luke's sincerity wasn't helped by the fact that she had only seen him at church on Sunday during the past two weeks. During those times, their conversations had been brief, almost too polite. Miserably Laney feared that Luke had changed his mind and just didn't know how to tell her. She took comfort from the fact that she would soon be at the ranch for Christmas Day and would get to the bottom of things.

After conferring with his father-in-law, Doc Simpson, Sam had concluded that whatever Pa's illness, it likely wasn't the contagious sort, so he okayed an outing for Christmas dinner.

Thankfully, though the air was icy, no snow fell on Christmas Day. Jane was beside herself with excitement over the new dress Laney and Granny had made her. Predictably Pa balked about going to the St. Johns', but Laney dug in her heels and refused to budge.

"You're going if I have to get Luke over here to carry you to the wagon. Besides, don't you want one last Christmas with Janey? Think of what it will mean to her."

Finally he relented and even agreed to a bath and a shave. Laney had bought him a new pair of britches and a nice warm flannel shirt at Tucker's. He seemed to perk up and didn't complain even once during the ride over.

Laney's palms grew damp as the ranch came into view. She hadn't seen Papa Dell since Thanksgiving; and at that time, he hadn't been out of bed yet, so she'd barely spoken to him. She knew he was sitting up for longer and longer periods of time now, and she hated the thought of having to face him. The guilt of her prayer that Luke would have to stay in Harper tore at her most of the time. She wanted desperately to confess, throw her arms around him, and beg his forgiveness, but deeper than her need to confess was her aversion to the thought of Papa Dell being disappointed in her.

Luke was on hand to greet her when the wagon rolled next to the house. "Merry Christmas," he said, his voice husky and filled with longing.

All at once, relief flooded Laney. The way Luke gazed at her was definitely the look of a man in love. At least that was one worry she could lay to rest today. Now if only she could put aside her guilt over Papa Dell as easily. She squared her shoulders and ascended the porch steps.

She grinned as Jane immediately went off to play with Cat, the youngest member of the St. John clan.

As gracious as ever, Mama Cassidy gave Jenkins the best chair in the house and insisted on giving him a quilt to lay across his lap. To Laney's amazement, her pa seemed honestly grateful as he snuggled under the covers and watched the comings and goings of the St. Johns.

Papa Dell sat in the chair opposite him and immediately struck up a conversation. Laney noticed her pa relax visibly, and she felt the tension leave her own shoulders, as well. Everything would be fine.

Thirty minutes later, Laney groaned to herself as Papa Dell called to her. How could she have thought everything would be fine? Luke had taken off without telling her where he was going or inviting her along, and once again, all of her earlier doubts began to surface.

Laney sat on the hearth, feeling the warmth from the fire heating up her backside.

"How are you doing?" Papa Dell asked, his eyes filled with genuine concern and love.

Unable to hold his gaze, Laney studied the scuff marks on the tips of her boots. "I'm fine," she mumbled.

"Glad to hear it. I know you've been mighty busy, but it's good to see you."

"Yeah, between Tucker's orders and now Pa and Jane . . ."

"I understand, believe me. Sometimes life

makes it impossible to find time for anything other than work and church meetings. I'm just glad you're with us today."

Laney could bear no more. Tears stung her eyes, and she laid her head on Papa Dell's lap. He hesitated briefly, then he stroked her hair.

"What is it, honey?" His voice sounded worried, his concern only fueling Laney's guilt.

"Oh, Papa Dell, I'm so sorry."

"What are you sorry about?"

"I did something terrible."

"I know you couldn't do anything truly bad, Laney."

"I did."

"Well, look at me and tell me what has you so upset."

She lifted her head from his lap but still couldn't bring herself to look at him. "I — I — Papa Dell . . . It's all my fault you got hurt."

"What do you mean? How could it possibly have been your fault?" Papa Dell cupped her chin and pressed gently until she had no choice but to look him in the eye.

Laney's stomach dropped. Now was the time for honesty. She couldn't put it off any longer. "I — I didn't want Luke to go out west, so I prayed for God to make a way for him to have to stay in Harper."

"And you think God answered your prayer by letting Ol' Angus tear into my leg?" He asked the question thoughtfully, and to Laney's relief, there was no anger in his tone.

"I reckon that's about the end of the matter, though I can't say how sorry I am about it. And if I could do it over, I'd just let Luke go and marry someone else. Honest, I would."

Papa Dell's lips twitched. "Those are some mighty powerful prayers you have there."

Laney nodded miserably. "I reckon I just have the praying touch. That was the first time I ever prayed for something for myself, Papa Dell, and look what happened. But don't worry, I'll never do it again."

"Well, don't give up on prayer altogether, honey. Do you think God would harm one of His children just to answer the prayers of another?"

"It appears that way."

Papa Dell gave her an indulgent smile. "Can you see me cutting off Luke's leg just to give Sam experience doctoring?"

" 'Course not!"

Papa Dell nodded. "God loves us the

same. And what happens to one of His children has nothing whatsoever to do with His answers to another."

"But . . . your leg . . ."

"My own stubbornness caused that accident. Luke told me a year ago we needed to sell Ol' Angus before he hurt someone. Since I let my pride stand in the way of a sound decision, I lost money putting Ol' Angus down, not to mention that now I have to wait until spring to buy another bull, and I'll lose out on one breeding cycle. My pride was pretty costly. But I promise, honey, this missing leg of mine isn't your fault."

Laney smiled. For the first time since the accident, the guilt lifted, and she felt almost giddy with relief. She threw her arms around Papa Dell. "Thank you."

"Now I expect to be seeing you a lot more around here. I need my dose of Laney every now and then to keep me laughing." He pulled his handkerchief from his pocket.

"I promise," she replied, accepting the proffered hanky.

The rattle of a wagon outside captured her attention. She turned to Papa Dell. "I didn't realize anyone else was coming."

"Yep," he said noncommittally.

A moment later, Luke burst in, his cheeks

red from the cold. He grinned at Laney. "Are you ready for your Christmas present?"

Laney's cheeks warmed. "I can't open my present before the kids!" What was Luke thinking?

He shrugged. "Have it your own way, but they'll get mighty cold standing on the porch until Christmas dinner is over and we gather round the tree."

"Honestly, Luke. What are you talking about?"

He stepped aside and swung open the door.

Laney gasped, shrieked, then flew into her brother's arms. "Ben! How'd you ever make it home on your preacher's salary?"

Then she gasped again at the rudeness of her question.

Ben laughed and lifted her into a crushing bear hug. "Papa Dell wrote us a letter, inviting us, and sent the tickets. We've been holed up at Tarah's since the train rolled in yesterday morning."

"I just can't believe you're here."

"What about me?" At one time Josie Raney's honeyed tone would have sent shivers of annoyance down Laney's spine, but now that she had made Ben so happy, Laney was willing to put aside past bad feelings and welcome her as a sister. Moving from Ben's arms to Josie's, Laney said, "Of course I'm thrilled to see you, too! You look downright beautiful."

Josie gave a pleasant laugh. "And you haven't changed one bit, Laney Jenkins. You're just as boyish as ever."

Laney stiffened. Maybe marrying Ben wasn't enough to redeem Josie after all. Laney felt a warm hand on her back and turned to find Luke grinning down at her.

"I hardly think anyone could call Laney boyish anymore." He chucked her chin. "She's too pretty for that."

Laney felt the warmth from her head to her toes. She could have hugged him right then and there and probably would have, if not for the sound of a raspy cough filling the air and silencing all banter and laughter — a reminder that Ben had a hurdle to get over before they could get on with their reunion.

"Ben, there's something you should —"

"It's all right, Laney. I knew he was here."

Ben moved slowly across the room, his limp more pronounced than Laney remembered. She started to follow, but the pressure of Luke's hand on her arm stopped her. Turning, she glowered at him, trying to jerk away, but he held firm.

"Let Ben handle this alone."

She nodded, and he loosened his grip, sliding his hand downward to grasp her hand. A delicious thrill shot through her, and she moved a step closer to him, enjoying the warmth of his arm pressed against hers.

"Hello, Pa," Ben said, his voice trembling slightly. Laney wondered if he was fighting for control or if he was truly glad to see their pa. Ben always was the more forgiving of them. Even when they had a chance to run away and live with Tarah, Ben had insisted they had to go home and honor Pa like the Bible said. Only days later, Pa had sold them to Anthony and Tarah — but by then, Ben had a black eye and bruised ribs from another undeserved beating.

Laney fought to control her anger at the memory. She wanted to rush forward and grab Ben away. He shouldn't be nice to Pa. The old rascal didn't deserve it.

Give him a good piece of your mind, Ben! She knew full well it wasn't in Ben's nature to hold a grudge — his marriage to Josie Raney was proof of that.

Pa's reply was short. "I see yer all growed up and probably think yer too good for yer ol' pa — just like her." Laney glared as he jerked a thumb at her.

Ben gave a good-natured chuckle. "True, I am all grown up, but no, I don't think I'm too good for my pa. As a matter of fact, I'd like you to meet someone." Ben turned and reached for his wife. Josie walked to him hesitantly, a tentative smile plastered on her face. Laney could tell she was fighting for her own control. The realization went a long way toward Laney's overlooking the earlier "boyish" comment.

"Least you got yerself a looker," Pa said with a knowing grin that made Josie blush to the roots of her blond hair.

Ben gathered her protectively around the shoulders and pulled her close. "She's beautiful on the outside, that's true, but her inward beauty is what made me fall head over heels in love with my wife."

Laney held back a snort. Boy, did Josie have her brother fooled.

Ben cleared his throat loudly and glanced about the room. "We actually have an announcement to make."

Laney waited impatiently. *Oh, please let him say he's moving back.*

"We just found out that God is blessing us with a new addition to the family. Looks like you're going to be a grandpa, Pa."

Pa squinted and eyed him for a moment. Laney hurried forward before Pa could ruin things with another crude comment and hugged Ben tightly. "Congratulations. Never thought I'd see the day you'd be a pa, but I know you'll be a good one." *A sight better than our own pa ever was.*

The family surrounded the happy couple, and for the next few minutes, the sitting room buzzed with congratulations, good-natured ribbing, and advice until Luke grabbed Laney's hand once again and cleared his throat. "I can't let Ben outdo me on Christmas," he said, grinning. "Laney and I have an announcement to make, too."

He paused long enough to search her face for approval. She smiled and nodded.

"Don't tell me ya got my daughter in a fix!"

Pa's outburst brought a collective gasp from the women. Laney would have gladly clobbered the old coot, but Luke squeezed her hand to silence her.

"Actually, our good news is that we're getting married."

"Finally!" Tarah stepped forward and grabbed them both, hugging them tightly. "I thought the two of you would never stop fighting long enough to actually realize you love each other."

The room exploded into laughter. The door opened, bringing a blast of cold inside as the children tromped in from their playing.

"We're starving," Little D complained. "Is the turkey done?"

"Little D," Anthony said, his tone taking on a rare sternness. "You're being impolite. I think you owe Grams an apology."

"Sorry, Grams," Little D muttered.

Cassidy sent the little guy a wink. "Accepted. And yes, the turkey will be coming out of the oven in just a few minutes, so you children get out of those wraps and come help us set the table."

Laney stepped forward to help Jane out of her coat and scarf. "There's someone I want you to meet," she whispered to the little girl.

She nestled her little sister in the crook of her arm and pulled her close, moving toward Ben. He apparently had been made aware of their new little sister, for his expression gentled.

"Ben, meet our little sister, Jane. Jane, this is our big brother, Ben. He came all the way from Virginia to meet you and to have Christmas dinner with us."

Josie gasped. "Why, she looks exactly like Laney!"

Jane and Laney glanced at each other and grinned. "Thank you," they replied in unison, then joined the laughter once again

164

filling the room.

Ben knelt down in front of the little girl. "It's nice to meet you, sweetheart. This is your new big sister, Josie. She's my wife."

"Hi," Jane said shyly, her eyes wide in admiration for Josie. A surge of jealousy shot through Laney, although she understood. As a young girl, she had looked upon Tarah with the same adoration. Jane loved frilly, dressy things, so it was only natural she'd admire Josie's beauty and ladylike manner.

"May I go help with the table settin'?" she asked Laney.

"Sure you can, honey."

Jane hurried to join the other children.

Laney sighed as she watched her go. "She's a wonderful little girl, Ben. Anyone would be proud to have her as a sister."

She felt the warmth of his arm as he pulled her to him. "You're quite a wonderful sister, too, Laney. I'm right proud of you. Let's go outside and talk for a few minutes."

Laney nodded. They grabbed their wraps and headed outside. No one asked where they were going or whether or not they wanted company. Everyone seemed to sense that the two needed a few minutes of privacy.

"It took a lot of gumption taking Pa in the

165

way you did, especially under the circumstances."

Laney leaned over the porch rail, resting her elbows on the rough wood. "You heard about him holing up at the soddy with those two varmints?"

Ben gave her a solemn nod. "I did. He looks pretty bad, doesn't he?"

"Sam says he's dying."

After a long silence, Laney turned to glance at Ben and straightened in shock to see tears streaming down his cheeks.

"What are you crying for?" But she knew. She had felt it, too. No matter how mean he'd been, he was their pa, and his soul was in danger of eternal darkness without Jesus.

"Oh, Laney. We can't let him die a sinner."

"I tried talking to him about Jesus one night," Laney said, defenses raised. "He told me to shut up."

"Don't give up on him. Jesus never gave up on us."

Sudden shame gripped Laney. All she'd been focused on was Pa's trial date so that he would leave her house. *Give me another chance, Lord, and I'll share with Pa about You.*

CHAPTER 11

Amid kisses and hugs, tears, and promises to keep in touch, Ben and Josie boarded the train for Virginia two weeks after Christmas. A month later, the sheriff finally brought the news that the circuit judge would make an appearance in Harper within three weeks' time.

Laney approached the day of reckoning with a combination of relief and dread. Pa was a difficult patient, at best. At worst, a trial by fire. His orneriness and deliberate jibes were almost more than she was willing to take. His only redeeming quality, as far as she could see, was that he loved little Jane. And the child loved him — the one fact that saved his scrawny carcass from being hauled into town and turned over to the sheriff for the duration.

Despite her guilty conscience, Laney tried to ignore him as much as possible. The task wasn't as simple as it seemed, for he wheezed and coughed all night until Laney was sure he did it on purpose just to spite her and keep her awake. When she was rested, she recognized the thought as ridiculous; but at three in the morning, after thrashing about all night, it was almost impossible to convince her sleep-deprived brain of anything that made sense.

"There now, that just about does it for this one." Granny smoothed the red satin gown and prepared to pack it for transport into town.

"Doesn't Miss DuPres wear the prettiest dresses?" Emily asked.

Laney glanced at the newly made gown, ordered from Tucker by the newest addition to the town — a singer named Vivienne, with raven hair and flawless skin that looked as though it had never seen a ray of sunshine. Laney thought she looked downright ghoulish; but the men in town, including Luke — much to Laney's annoyance — seemed to think her quite becoming. Laney regretted allowing Emily and Luke to talk her into going to the schoolhouse the previous night to listen to the indecent woman. It was a waste of good money when she could listen to Anthony sing hymns on Sunday morning for free.

Emily had stopped by early this morning

168

to discuss the concert. To Laney's irritation, her adopted sister was mesmerized by the singer's "charm and beauty" and raved until Laney wanted to throw her out of the house — but to do so would be an admission of jealousy, and Laney Jenkins wasn't jealous of anyone.

So she sat pushing her needle through the fabric while Granny finished up the red silk and Emily sipped tea — for coffee was now simply too crude a drink for a lady — and talked nonstop about the lovely and wonderful Miss Vivienne DuPres.

"If only I didn't have this horrible red hair and freckles," Emily lamented for what seemed like the twentieth time in as many minutes. "Miss DuPres says all the really famous singers have perfectly white skin and hair as soft as silk."

Laney gave a loud snort but continued to work, hemming Louisa Kirkpatrick's latest gown, a replica of a gown she saw in *Godey's Lady's Book* and designed specifically to keep Louisa firmly in the seat of fashion superiority, regardless of the newest woman in town.

"Did you say something, Laney?" Emily asked.

"Nah."

Granny cackled. "What have you got

against Miss DuPres?"

Laney turned and stared hard at Granny. How did the old woman always seem to know what she was thinking? "I don't have anything against *Vivienne.* I don't even know her. I just think Emily should be happy with the looks God gave her and stop trying to look like some floozy saloon girl."

Emily gasped. Laney cut her a glance and noted with concern that, between the freckles, her face was every bit as pale as Vivienne's.

"Laney Jenkins, you take that back," Emily declared hotly, the color returning to her face and going beyond natural to an angry pink. "Miss DuPres is as decent a woman as you or I. And she is *not* a s—saloon girl. You know very well she is a wonderful singer using her talent to support herself. Furthermore, if Pa and the rest of the town council, *including* our preacher, think there's nothing improper with her singing in town, then I don't see how you have the right to call her names. So there!"

Laney blinked in surprise at the outburst. She shrugged and tried to pretend she didn't care that Emily was defending an interloper. "Honestly. Don't get in a snit about it. I'm sorry I said anything." She glanced back at her sewing. "But I got a

170

right to my opinion," she mumbled.

A coughing laugh sounded from the bed. "Yer just jealous, girlie. What's a matter? That man of yourn cast sheep eyes at a woman pertier and softer than you?"

Laney eyed the shears and debated the consequences, then decided to stab him with the truth instead. "Luke doesn't cast 'sheep eyes,' " she declared through gritted teeth. "And especially not at some floo—" She cast a cautious glance at Emily. "Especially not at another woman. Not all men are like *some* men." She gave him a pointed look.

Rising on his elbow, he pointed a shaky finger and gave her a squinty-eyed glare. "One man's just like another, and you best find that out sooner than later, girl. Yer precious 'Lukey' would leave for greener pastures if he could, and you know it. Yer gonna be mighty lucky if he sticks around after yer all fat and have two or three young'uns hanging off yer dress."

"Oh, hush up and lay back down, you old fool," Granny commanded. "Don't compare my grandson with the likes of you."

"You tryin' to tell me he didn't give up his plans to go west because his pa had an amputation? You don't think he'll hightail it to Oregon just as soon as that ranch is off his neck?"

Now how did he know all about Luke's plans? The old eavesdropper! Still, his words rang with a smidgen of truth, bringing Laney's fears back to the surface.

As Granny launched into a list of Luke's attributes, thereby proving his superior character, Laney pondered her pa's words.

What if Luke did decide he couldn't go through with the marriage?

The sun filtered in through the window, causing the ring on Laney's left hand to glimmer. She didn't need the garnet ring, which Luke had presented to her on her birthday the day after Christmas. A wedding band on the day they said their vows would have been enough, but Luke had insisted. He loved her that much, she thought with a sense of satisfaction. "No, Luke wouldn't leave. He gave me his word." She jerked her head in surprise. She hadn't meant to speak. Heat flooded her face as Pa gave her a knowing grin, which clearly asked the same question she'd been pondering for the past few weeks: Did she want to keep Luke here because of a promise? If she held him to it, would he resent her forever and wish they'd never married? Laney knew she couldn't live with that, but could she live without Luke if she released him from his promise?

Returning her attention to her sewing, she tried to push the thoughts aside but found she kept returning to the troublesome issue. Luke was doing a fine job of running the ranch, and they all looked forward to the four expected foals and many calves due this spring.

Papa Dell still struggled to walk with the use of crutches he had carved for himself while sitting before the fire day after day. Though all were thrilled with his progress and he seemed in better spirits since he could get around on his own, everyone knew that hobbling with crutches was a far cry from sitting a horse and running a ranch.

So, for now, Luke seemed to have resigned himself to the task at hand, which allowed Laney to push aside her fears. But she knew sooner or later, Papa Dell would be fully healed, learn to ride again with a missing leg, and take over. The question was, would Luke be content to stay in Harper, or would he keep his promise, marry her, and regret it for the rest of his life?

Laney pulled on the reins to make Colby walk calmly next to the wagon. On the wagon seat, Luke held the reins while

Granny sat primly next to him, her back straight, gaze forward, hands folded in her lap. Anticipation shone in her faded gray eyes. Laney grinned. Mr. Tucker would be happy to see her, as well.

She cast her glance to the back of the wagon. Pa sat up, determined he would not ride to his court hearing lying in the back of a wagon like some invalid. Jane sat next to him.

Luke reined in the team in front of Tucker's and hopped down to help Granny from the wagon. Laney dismounted Colby and tethered him to the hitching post. She glanced in the back of the wagon. "Jane, honey, can you please stay here and keep Pa company while we go inside and attend to business?"

The child smiled her missing-tooth smile and nodded. "We'll play a game. Won't we, Pa?"

"A game?" He scowled, but after seeing the child's sudden pout, the harsh lines in his face softened. "What sorta game?"

Laney and Luke exchanged a smile at Pa's expense while Luke grabbed the crate containing the finished gowns. Granny preceded them up the steps to the mercantile. Laney nudged Luke when the older woman stopped at the door and patted her bonnet in the window reflection, as though patting her bonnet would straighten any mussed hair beneath its cloth folds. She touched the cameo clasped at her collar before opening the door and stepping inside.

"Think those two will ever tie the knot?" Luke asked.

Laney gave a short laugh. "I wouldn't be surprised if they make it to the altar before we do."

"Don't count on it," he said, capturing her gaze. Laney gulped at the hunger burning in his eyes. She thought he might kiss her right in front of the whole town of Harper, but a honey-toned call from the road caught their attention.

"Oh my goodness. Hold the door, please."

Laney turned to see who had ruined her moment and fought back a biting comment as Miss DuPres joined them — out of breath from running ten feet in a dress pulled so tight in the middle that Laney was surprised she was conscious, let alone walking and talking.

Luke stood before the door, holding the crate and, to Laney's chagrin, gaping at Vivienne like an imbecile.

"Move out of the way so I can open the door, Luke," she grumped, pushing him aside as roughly as she could and wishing she could just flatten him right then and there.

"I declare, it's an absolute gale out here. My hair will be down any moment."

"Seems pretty calm to me," Laney observed just as a gust of wind nearly knocked her off her feet. "Maybe you oughtta use more pins in your hair if you need to have it in all sorts of twists and curls." Laney thought it was just about the dumbest hairstyle she'd ever seen — much too loose for a March day in Kansas. A long braid down the back was the only way to keep hair from flying and falling during spring weather. Some women just plain weren't as smart as they were pretty — not that she thought Vivienne pretty.

"Why, thank you. What a wonderful suggestion," Miss DuPres replied, beaming at Laney as though she had just elected her president. "I'll just pick up some more pins while I'm here."

Stunned into silence, Laney stepped aside while Miss DuPres glided between Luke — who still couldn't seem to find his tongue — and Laney, who was just about to suggest he go wait in the wagon. Miss DuPres's lavender scent drifted between them. Laney noticed Luke swallow and raise his brow to Laney. "She's something, isn't she?"

"Yeah, she is." *A fancy-pants, powder-wearing, toilet water-drenched, man-stealing floozy.* And Laney wasn't going to put up with it. She'd rather lose Luke to the westward fever than have him trapped by dangly eardrops and low-cut gowns.

With purpose, she punched Luke's arm — a little harder than necessary — to gain his attention.

"What was that for?"

"Stop gawking at the singer. You're holding up the door. We're going to be late for Pa's hearing."

"Who's gawking?" Luke turned red and maneuvered the large crate through the doorway.

"You are," she replied with a huff.

"Well, it ain't like *that*. So stop being all green-eyed. I just haven't ever seen anyone so . . . I don't know . . . like her."

Laney knew what he meant, even if he didn't. Miss DuPres was exactly the "ideal woman" Luke had described right before that fateful kiss. But there was no way she was going to bring that up and remind him that she would never be the type of woman he truly wanted.

When they reached the counter, Vivienne took her red gown and held it up against herself. She glowed with excitement. "It's just the most beautiful thing I've ever laid eyes on." Her eyes shone with admiration as she regarded Laney. "And you make gowns like this all the time? Why, you'd make a fortune in the city."

Maybe the lady isn't quite so bad, Laney conceded.

"Whoa now, little lady," Tucker growled. "We got us a deal. Don't be puttin' ideas in that girl's head. If she thought she could make a dime, she'd ride four days on a half-dead pony and scoop up cow patties."

Miss DuPres giggled. "Well, I suppose I would, too, Mr. Tucker. A lady has to make a living somehow. We can teach, sing, or find work as a seamstress if we have the gift for it. And my, oh my, miss, you have the touch."

Laney cleared her throat. "Thanks," she mumbled. "It's nothing."

"Nothing? Oh, Miss . . . what is your name?"

"Laney."

"Well, Miss Laney. This is absolutely the best seamstress work I've ever seen in my life. Oh, if only I . . ."

Her face suddenly turned just about as red as the gown, and she turned to Mr. Tucker. "I — I don't know how to tell you this, sir, but . . . Well, it's just that my manager, you know the man I traveled with? He . . ." Her face crumbled, and she burst into tears — not the delicate tears one would expect from a dainty woman of refinement.

Tucker's gaze swept Granny, Laney, and Luke, horror smoothing the age lines extending from the corners of his eyes to his cheeks. "There, there, miss," he said awkwardly, his expression going from horror to horrified pleading.

Granny came to his rescue and stepped forward. Tucker gladly moved aside, faster than Laney ever would have thought him capable of moving.

"Now, honey, tell us what's wrong."

Vivienne swiped the back of her hand across her nose.

"Luke," Granny said, "give the poor girl your hanky."

Luke cleared his throat and fished his hanky out of his pocket. "Here, Miss Du-Pres," he said, extending the handkerchief.

"Thank you," she gulped out. Rather than patting the cloth daintily against her nose, Miss DuPres gave several hearty blows while the onlookers waited for her explanation.

Finally she gave a nervous little laugh and glanced around. "Goodness, I've certainly made a spectacle of myself, haven't I?"

Laney had to agree, but she also had to admit it made her like the singer a little more. A little, but not much.

"Why don't you tell us what's wrong?" she said impatiently.

Miss DuPres chewed her lip. "I really . . . well, you're strangers; I don't know if I should . . ."

"Well, that's about the end of it, then," Laney said. She turned to Tucker. "How's about settling up so we can get to the schoolhouse? The judge is meeting us there for Pa's hearing today."

"Well — well, wait just a minute."

Laney cast a glance at Miss DuPres. "Something wrong?"

"Well, it's just that . . . I didn't say I *wouldn't* tell you what was wrong. I just didn't know if I *should* or not."

A shrug lifted Laney's shoulders. "We don't have to know your private business. But if you're done crying, don't forget to give Luke back his handkerchief. I made that for him. He's my fiancé," she said.

"Oh, well, I had a fiancé, too."

Oh, great. Laney could have kicked herself as fat tears once more began to roll down flawless cheeks.

"Is that what has you all upset, honey?"

Granny asked.

Miss DuPres nodded.

Granny glanced at Tucker. "She needs another hanky."

The old man pulled a handkerchief from his pocket.

"Not a used one!"

Tucker looked helplessly around, then heaved a sigh and pulled one off the shelf. He mumbled something about folks thinking he was made of money, until a glare from Granny silenced him. "No charge."

"How kind!" Vivienne's splotchy face brightened for a second, then fell again.

"Now, about this fiancé . . ." Laney had just about had all the delays she could handle, and if this Miss DuPres didn't share her troubles soon, she could just forget all about it.

"Are you sure you don't mind listening?"

"Of course we don't mind," Luke soothed, much to Laney's irritation.

"Why else would we have asked?" she said roughly.

Vivienne heaved a great sigh and finally launched her tale of woe. "My Randy heard me singing through the door of my room at his mother's boardinghouse back in Chicago. I declare, the moment I saw him, I fell head over heels in love. Imagine my joy

181

when he proposed. I would have married him right away, but he said he wanted me to have the wedding of my dreams, and we would get married as soon as we saved enough money for a silk gown and a big fat diamond for my finger. Before long, we started traveling to other towns. I sang everywhere." She glanced at Granny a little fearfully. "Some of the places we went weren't very Christian, ma'am."

"That's in the past now," Granny assured her with a comforting pat on her arm.

She sniffed and covered Granny's veined hand with her own. "Thank you."

Laney tossed a glance at the ceiling and sighed heavily. "Then what?"

"Excuse me?" A blank gaze captured Laney's. "Oh. You mean, then what happened with Randy. Well, we finally came here to wonderful Harper, where everyone has been so amazingly kind, coming to hear me sing. We collected more money than ever, and I just knew we had finally saved enough to get married properly. B–but last night I brought it up, and Randy grew quite angry and said we had to wait until we got back to Chicago because his mother would be very hurt unless she could attend her only child's wedding. And truly, I understood. So I told him that was just fine.

B–but this morning when I walked downstairs, the hotel clerk told me . . . that is, he said that Randy . . ." She let out a pitiful wail and covered her face with her hands. "I'm so humiliated! How on earth could he do this to me?"

"What is it?" Granny asked, and even Laney had to admit she was a mite curious herself.

"Randy ran off with all the money!" Great sobs engulfed her body, and she clung to Granny. "He didn't even pay the hotel bill, and now the owner is threatening to call in the sheriff. I — I can't buy the gowns I ordered, Mr. Tucker. But if you'll please just not press charges, I'll try to find work here in Harper, and I'll pay you every red cent."

"Well now, how am I supposed to stay in business if people don't pay for what they order?"

"Honestly, Tuck," Laney heard herself say. "It's not like she did it on purpose. You heard her promise to pay you. Don't you think she's been through enough?"

"Leave the poor girl alone," Luke said. "Miss DuPres didn't steal from you. She can't help what happened."

"Of course Mr. Tucker will wait for the money," Granny soothed. "And if the gowns sell before you pay him back, of course you won't owe him anything."

Tucker gave Granny a look that clearly said he thought she'd lost her mind, but like a man in love, he smiled and nodded. "That's right, miss. You just don't worry about it. I can hardly keep ready-made dresses in stock. Them three dresses you ordered'll sell lickety-split."

"Two dresses," Granny corrected. "The red dress would never suit another woman. Wrap it up, Tucker. You can take our commission off, and Miss DuPres will owe you only for the material."

"What?" Now it was Laney's turn to stare. "Granny!"

"No, I couldn't. Honest. It isn't necessary. I don't need a new gown."

"Yes, you do," Granny insisted. "You are going to be singing again next week, and you need a new gown."

"But everyone has already come to hear me, ma'am. In a town this size, I can only get one, maybe two performances until I lose money."

"Nonsense. God will provide. And you'll come back to the ranch with me to stay until you have the money to move on."

"I just don't know what to say." Vivienne's eyes filled again.

You could say no, Laney thought ungraciously.

"I have no choice but to accept. I just hope you won't regret it."

Laney spun around and stomped to the door. She jerked it open and slammed it shut behind her. That floozy! Weaseling her way into Luke's family's ranch. Laney wouldn't stand for it. No siree.

Planting her hands on her hips, she glanced around the town and tried to gain her composure. What else could go wrong today? Then, with a groan, she remembered the hearing. They were five minutes late.

CHAPTER 12

Laney's nerves remained taut while the judge listened to the witness seated on his left, his fingers pressed thoughtfully against his graying temple. The prosecutor waxed eloquent, and Laney had to admit if she were the judge, she'd lock up her pa and throw away the key.

She glanced at Mr. Carpenter, the businessman who had been robbed, as he sat on the makeshift witness stand, answering question after question about the awful night three men had invaded his home while he and his family slept only a few rooms away.

He had awakened to the noise of the prowlers and gone to investigate. When he confronted the three men, one of the robbers — Matt, Laney surmised, from the description — fired his weapon and shot the man right in the arm. He still had nightmares about it. And would the judge please make the men pay back his money?

When all was said and done, Pa was found guilty. Laney felt a sense of relief as the judge pronounced a sentence of life in prison rather than hanging. Still, one look at Pa's sickly face, and she knew he wouldn't last a week in prison — even a mild one. As the judge raised his gavel to finalize his sentence, Laney scrambled to her feet.

"Excuse me, Your Honor."

The judge glanced up. "What can I do for you, miss?"

Laney slowly made her way to the front of the schoolhouse. "I appreciate you going easy on my pa. I guess some folks feel like he deserves to hang for stealing a man's hard-earned money. I'm trying to buy a little piece of land and a soddy myself, so I can surely understand their way of thinking. But you see . . ." She cleared her throat and gazed directly into the bewildered judge's eyes. "The thing is, my pa's a very sick man. He's not going to be around much longer as it is, so sending him to prison will be a waste of time. I was thinking maybe you'd just let him come home with me so he can spend the rest of his days with me taking care of him. And don't worry. If he gets well — which Sam says he won't — I'll send him straight to the sheriff so he can take his punishment fair and square."

"I'm sorry." The judge leaned toward her, confusion clouding his eyes. "What are you asking me?"

"Can he come home with me?" What kind of smarts did it take to be a judge, anyway?

"Let me get this straight," Judge Campbell said with a firmness that made Laney squirm. "You would like for me to suspend your father's sentence and allow him to go home with you instead of to prison."

"Yes, sir."

"I'm afraid that just isn't —"

Laney leaned over the teacher's desk the judge was using as his bench. She dropped her tone so that the occupants of the small room couldn't hear. "Are you a Christian, Your Honor?"

"Now don't start using my faith against me," he said, giving her a stern frown. "Your father must pay for his crime."

"Yes, sir. I know what he did was wrong. But he only has a short time to live, under the best of conditions. If you send him to prison, he'll die in a godless, sinful state. And you know where sinners go when they die. Can you send a sinful man to his death?"

"I certainly can," hc said. "The matter is settled." He raised the gavel again.

A sense of urgency tugged at Laney, and she grabbed the judge's arm. "Wait!"

"I beg your pardon."

"Please. Won't you consider my suggestion? What good will it do to send him to prison? He'll be dead in a month if you do."

The judge glanced at her thoughtfully for a moment, then opened his mouth as though ready to relent.

"Excuse me, Your Honor."

The judge sighed heavily. "Yes?"

Laney turned to find Mr. Carpenter approaching the judge. "I will see this man punished for his crime. My family lost a great deal of money that he took and squandered for his own pleasure. He must be made to pay."

An idea formed in Laney's mind, and she addressed the wronged man. "How much did my pa and his partners take from you?"

She started at the amount. "If I give you my pa's cut of your money" — she turned to the judge — "then will you consider it?"

"If restitution is made, I could possibly consider your request, under the circumstances."

"But that's only a third of what was taken from me." The man's whine was beginning to irritate Laney. "I will not stand for it!" He pounded his fist on the desk. "I'll take it to a higher court. I'll write to the governor."

The judge glanced from Mr. Carpenter to Laney. "I'm sorry, miss. This isn't worth the headache to me. My decision stands." For a third time, he raised his gavel.

"Wait. One more thing." Laney gritted her teeth, unable to believe she was about to voice the thoughts twisting through her mind. "I will pay Mr. Carpenter everything my pa and those two no-good scoundrels stole, if you'll only allow him to come home and die in peace."

The judge cast a questioning glance at Mr. Carpenter. "How's that sound to you? The girl pays you the money, I let Jenkins go home to die, and you drop the whole thing and don't raise a fuss about it."

The man rocked on his heels and screwed up his face as though considering the proposition, but Laney could tell by the gleam in his eye that he had already made up his mind.

"I can accept that."

"Good. It's done." The judge slammed the gavel down on the desk before anyone else could interrupt. "And if by some miracle that scoundrel happens to recover, I don't want to hear about it."

Relief coursed through Laney. "I'll head over to the bank right now." She spun on her heel and walked down the aisle toward the door. Luke rose as though he would follow, but she waved him back to his seat. She glared at Pa on the way out. *God forgive me, but I think I hate him. After all the low-down things he's done in his life, now he's off the hook, and I'm paying all I have to buy his freedom.*

She dashed a tear from her cheek. Mr. Garner wouldn't be getting a large lump sum of money after all. Her loan payment was due tomorrow, but there wasn't any possible way she could pay. She would lose her dream.

For the first time, she truly understood how Luke felt about not going west.

Pa wasn't even grateful! Laney kicked at a pebble, sending it sailing into the rippling creek. The cantankerous, ungrateful swindler didn't even care what she had sacrificed to give him a little more time on this earth! Disappointment swelled her chest, threatening to spill over in hot tears.

One month, Garner had said. One month to raise the money to make up for the payment she owed him plus the payment due at the end of that amount of time.

Even with Granny's help, she couldn't work hard enough to raise the money. She sat hard on the damp prairie earth that only now was beginning to turn green with the promise of an early spring. Hugging her knees to her chest, Laney gave a weary sigh and rested her chin on her arms.

A cool, gentle breeze played with the loose tendrils around her face and brought the fresh scents of budding wildflowers to her nostrils, but she found no pleasure in the small reminder that all things were becoming new once again on the prairie. To Laney, all that was new and promising in her life had been taken away with the money she'd handed over to Mr. Carpenter.

Her mind raced with the possibilities of what she could do to save her soddy. She already knew Mr. Thomas at the bank wouldn't extend her a loan, because she had tried that before, asking Garner to carry the note.

Suddenly she lifted her chin, her eyes growing wide at the possibility of the forming idea. What about Luke? He had mentioned before that he had money saved. Laney's heart raced. That was the solution. This was to be their land after all.

Of course she couldn't ask him for the money. But Luke knew what she had done. Once he realized the implications of paying back what Pa had stolen, he would surely offer the money, and they would have their land.

She smiled for the first time in two days, took a deep cleansing breath, and stood. She wouldn't lose her land after all.

Luke stood on the front porch of the St. John ranch and gaped at Pa, unable to believe what he was actually hearing. "Are you telling me you want me to go?"

Pa nodded. "There's a wagon train pulling into Council Grove in a couple of months. You have plenty of time to get things settled here — marry Laney, get to Council Grove, and get outfitted before they pull out."

"But what about the ranch? You can't . . ."

"Hired Floyd Henderson today to manage the place. He was about to pull up stakes and head back east until I convinced him to stay and run the ranch for me. I'm happy with my decision. Now you're free, Luke. You've done more for me than I can say, and I appreciate it. But I can't let you sacrifice your plans for me."

"I don't know what to say, Pa. I just assumed . . ."

"That you were stuck here running the ranch?"

Luke couldn't deny it, so he said nothing.

"Nothing wrong with wanting to follow your own dreams. Nothing wrong with it at all." He clapped Luke on the shoulder and hobbled into the house, leaving Luke to stare after him.

An hour later, Luke looked across the pasture, his arms resting on the fence he had built just last week. He heaved a sigh. Everything changed so fast. First he was making plans to go west, only to have those plans upset. Then just as quickly, when he'd resigned himself to never making it to Oregon, Pa offered him the chance to live the life he wanted.

A thrill passed through him as all the dreams he'd stuffed down now sprang to the surface. He thought of plush green fields, acres and acres of cattle grazing on his land. A log home that Laney would be proud to tend. He saw children — his and Laney's — running and playing about the place.

Laney. Her image in his mind jolted him back to the present. What would she say? Reality broke through as he anticipated her response. She wouldn't leave Harper. Especially now that her pa and Jane were counting on her. He had made her a promise. Had proposed twice. How could he ask her once more to release him from his promise to marry her? Luke felt pressure overtake him like a ton of water carrying him away against his will.

He couldn't imagine life without Laney. He couldn't imagine life without trying to fulfill his dream. The question he needed answered was, which could he live without the easiest? He knew he couldn't have both.

"It's a lovely piece of land, Luke."

Luke started and turned sharply at the sound of Vivienne's soft voice. He felt the intrusion clench his gut, and he wished he could ask her to leave him alone.

"It is pretty land," he replied. "There's lots of pretty land in the country."

"I heard your pa telling your ma that you're thinking of heading west."

"That's right."

"You won't find anything better, no matter where you run to."

"Maybe. Maybe not."

She placed a gentle hand upon his arm. "There's no maybe about it. Here you have your wonderful family, a woman who loves you and wants to marry you, a town where you're respected. You're extremely blessed."

Luke turned, regarding her thoughtfully. Were Vivienne's observations an answer from God about what he was supposed to do, or was she just butting in? If only he could be sure that whatever decision he made was the right one.

"What will you do, Miss DuPres?" he asked, if for no other reason than to push aside his own quandary for a while and focus on something else.

She shrugged. "Your granny thinks my performance Friday night will be a success. If only it will provide me with the funds to go someplace new. Maybe someplace back east. Or maybe . . ." She cut her glance to his. "Maybe I should go west and see what Oregon has to offer a singer. What do you think? Could you use some company on the trip west?"

Luke swallowed hard. How was he supposed to get out of this without offending a lady or making Laney hate him?

Miss DuPres laughed and gave his arm a playful tap. "Don't worry, Luke. You're too young for me. Besides, I hear in Oregon there are ten men to every woman. I'd have my pick."

A sheepish grin tipped Luke's mouth. "I bet you'd have your pick of men no matter where you go, Miss DuPres."

"Why, thank you. What a sweet thing to say!"

Before he could stop her, Miss DuPres rose up on her toes and gave him a fat kiss right on his cheek. Luke felt his ears burn. He could have taken a little embarrassment. What he couldn't take was the sound of Laney's roar behind him or the look of utter rage on her face when he turned around to face her.

"Luke St. John!" she hollered at the top of her voice. "You . . . I . . . I can't believe . . ."

This was one time Luke was grateful that the angrier Laney became, the smaller her vocabulary.

"Simmer down," he said, knowing full well she wouldn't. "This isn't anything for you to be jealous about."

"Jealous? Ha." She snorted. "You'll never see a day you can make me jealous."

"There's been a misunderstanding." Miss DuPres stepped forward, her tone conciliatory, if slightly fearful. "It's all my fault. If you'll only let me explain."

"You stay out of this," Laney commanded. "The first time my back is turned, he goes and kisses another woman just because she's all soft and womanly. For shame, Luke. How could you go making cow eyes at someone else?"

"I wasn't making cow eyes at anyone. As a matter of fact, she kissed me. What did you want me to do, knock her flat?"

"I would have!"

"Oh my." Vivienne pressed her hand to her bosom, looking as though she might faint any minute.

"Honestly," Laney said, sending her a look of utter disdain. "I wouldn't hit you. I meant if a man kissed me, I'd knock him flat."

"You never knocked me flat for kissing you." Luke moved in closer and took her hands in his.

She jerked away, her face growing pink. "You know what I mean, and don't try to sweet-talk your way out of this."

"Really, Laney," Vivienne pleaded. "Allow me to defend this gentleman's honor."

"Gentleman," Laney said with a sniff. She crossed her arms across her chest. "Fine. Make it quick."

"Very well. First of all, he's telling the truth. He didn't kiss me. I kissed *him*. And not because I have some dream of snatching him away from you. I kissed him out of gratitude because he offered me a few kind words — words that a woman needs to hear after she's been lied to, robbed, and abandoned. Your wonderful Luke merely spoke kindly to me. But you have more than his words, you silly girl. You have his love forever." Vivienne walked past them. She gave Laney a pat on the arm without slow-ing her gait. "I hope you will appreciate the treasure he is offering you," she called over her shoulder as she made her way back toward the house.

"Well, that was some speech." Laney looked up at him. "I guess I acted a little drastically, didn't I?"

"You must be growing up," Luke said with a chuckle. He swept her around the waist and pulled her close. "I expected a lot worse."

She laughed and punched his chest. "I could always flatten you now."

"I'd rather get a kiss."

She tilted her head and smiled, the look of love in her eyes clouding his senses. Desperation surged inside of him, and he captured her lips, drinking deeply of their softness. He held her tightly, afraid he might lose her if he loosened his grip. Over and over, he kissed her until she wilted against him.

Laney pulled slightly away. "Luke," she breathed against his lips.

Without answering, he covered her mouth once again. He couldn't lose her. He wouldn't!

Not until Laney cried out did he loosen his hold.

"Luke, stop it. You're hurting me!"

He released her suddenly, nearly knocking them both off their feet. Laney gasped and stared at him in bewildered silence. She touched her fingers to her lips.

"Say something, Laney," he said, his voice hoarse.

"I don't understand." She rammed her hands onto her hips, her stance indicating she was ready for a fight. "You'd better explain right now, because I don't plan on being manhandled. Not even by my husband."

He groaned inwardly at the thought of her thinking he would ever purposely hurt her. "I'm sorry, honey." He reached for her, but she quickly stepped away from his arms.

"Don't pull away, please. I don't know what came over me. Forgive me."

"Just don't ever be that rough with me again, Luke. I mean it." Laney's expression softened, and she moved back into his arms.

Relief surged over Luke. "I love you," he whispered and brushed his lips across the top of her head.

"I love you, too, Lukey," she murmured against his chest. "I'll always love you."

They fell silent and watched the sun sink into a glorious orange sky. "Isn't it beautiful?" Laney asked.

"Mmm."

"Just think about all the sunsets we'll watch together for the rest of our lives, Luke."

He knew he should tell her he was thinking about the move west again — give her the chance to rail at him. But he couldn't. Not now. Resting his cheek against the silky softness of her hair, he drank in her sweet smell and knew he'd never watch another sunset as lovely as this one.

CHAPTER 13

A sense of foreboding gnawed at Laney as she and Luke walked arm in arm toward the house. That was not a mere kiss of passion from a man more than ready to be married. It was something more. Fear railed against reason. What was wrong with Luke? He had gone from passionate to gentle to sullen in the span of thirty minutes. Now she couldn't drag two words out of him.

She had asked him what was wrong, but he insisted everything was fine. He wasn't being honest, and Laney didn't like it one bit. A horrid thought wormed into her mind. What if Luke's mood had to do with a certain Miss DuPres? She was everything Luke had admitted he thought a woman should be. Soft. Womanly. Someone a man could take care of. Laney could just bet that Miss DuPres would never even be tempted to lead a dance. The woman was as curvy as a winding road, too. A man couldn't help but admire that. Laney cast an unhappy glance down at her own figure. She had about as many curves as little Jane.

Before they even reached the house, they were greeted by the heavenly smells of roast beef and freshly baked bread. Laney's mouth watered. Pa had refused to come to supper, so Laney had warmed up yesterday's stew, grabbed Jane, and left him to sulk on his pallet while they were gone.

Guilt pricked her at the thought of him all alone, slurping warmed stew, but she quickly pushed it aside. After all, she thought bitterly, she had given everything for him — even though he surely didn't deserve it. Couldn't she enjoy one dinner with her fiancé and the family without his sourness weaseling in to ruin it for her?

And she tried. How she tried to enjoy the time around the St. John table — like old times. Customary laughter prevailed over the supper table, and the loving looks that passed between Mama Cassidy and Papa Dell filled Laney with longing. How could two people love and laugh so perfectly? She knew the story of Mama Cassidy and Emily coming to Papa Dell by wagon train and how the first few months were difficult between Mama Cassidy and Papa Dell. But looking at them now, no one would guess they hadn't always been in love. Mama Cassidy had shared with Laney once that sometimes love was hard-hitting and fast, snatching your breath away like a sudden wind. And sometimes it happened slowly over the years. Hers and Dell's, she'd said, was like a twister. It came suddenly and brought with it all sorts of disasters until God's peace calmed their storms.

Laney glanced at Luke from the corner of her eye. Theirs was a slow love. It had grown from friendship and had almost slipped by unnoticed. But the way Luke was acting now, she worried that perhaps he had decided he didn't feel any kind of love at all. Was his odd kiss similar to the one she had given him last year? Some sort of test? Maybe she had failed. A gasp escaped her. What if he didn't want to raise Jane? Or have to put up with her sickly pa?

Luke turned and caught her perusal. He winked, smiled, and captured her hand under the table. Laney smiled, and for a while her fears calmed once again.

Luke gripped Laney's tiny hand, careful not to hold too tightly. Desperation clawed at him, and he feared Vivienne or someone else would mention Oregon at any moment. He intended to speak with Laney soon, but not yet. He glanced at her practically untouched plate and willed her to hurry and finish so he could usher her out of the house before someone spoke up.

"Not hungry?" he asked.

"Hmm? Oh. I guess not."

"Are you feeling all right, Laney?" Ma's all-knowing gaze studied her. "You are looking a mite peaked. Are you working too hard again?"

Relief overtook Luke. If Ma started in on Laney about working too hard and not eating enough, he was safe from anyone bringing up his own dreaded topic before he could discuss it with her.

Laney gave Ma a half smile. "No, ma'am. I'm fine. Just not very hungry. Although the food is marvelous."

Granny harrumphed from her place directly across the table from Laney. "Don't you think I'd make her rest if we were working too hard? That was the whole point of my helping out over there."

"Of course, Granny," Ma said, her cheeks going pink. "I didn't mean to imply you were remiss in your duty to our Laney."

Luke's heart soared when Laney squeezed his hand and grinned at him during the exchange between Granny and Ma.

"I should say not. Besides, if she's peaked, it's not because Mr. Tucker's overworking her. It's because of that pa of hers."

Jane gasped, and Granny cut her a glance. "I'm sorry, Jane. I know we had a bargain, but you know your pa can be quite a trial for Laney."

Luke noticed that the little girl looked ready to argue, then her face softened, and she nodded. "Yes, ma'am. I reckon you're right." She screwed up her face. "But he ain't no rascal!"

"Well, we won't argue about that. Now you children finish your supper. Granny has some licorice sticks Mr. Tucker sent home with me last week."

Cat, Hope, Will, and Jane shared smiles among themselves and went about cleaning their plates.

Luke was just beginning to relax back into the comfort of his family when Vivienne spoke up. "Speaking of your pa, will he travel west, too, Laney?"

Laney gave her a blank stare. "Why would my pa go west? He can barely go to the out— well, he can barely get out of bed — although he does seem to be feeling a mite better these days. But not nearly well enough to travel. I suppose he'll stay with me until . . ." Her gaze darted to her sister. "He'll stay with me," she finished.

"I see. So you'll be joining Luke in Oregon . . ." She followed Laney's example and darted a glance at Jane. "Afterward?"

Luke wanted to slip under the table and slither outside unnoticed, now that Miss DuPres had opened up the topic he most feared. Why hadn't he just talked it over with Laney while he'd had the chance?

"Oregon? How did you know about that? Besides, Luke already decided not to go."

Vivienne's face brightened. "Good for you, Luke! You took my advice after all. I told you, this is a wonderful place to lay down roots and start a family."

"*Your* advice?" Laney said.

Luke squirmed while Laney glanced at him, then turned a scowl on Miss DuPres. "Luke decided not to go west months ago, before he even met *you*."

Pa cleared his throat. Thankfully Luke turned his attention toward the head of the table. "Have you decided for sure not to head west, son? I can always keep you on as manager and pay Floyd what I promised him just to stay on as a hand. Unless you and Laney have decided to go ahead and try to build your own herd. You let me know if I can help."

"Oh, Luke," Ma said, tears choking her voice. "I'm so relieved. I couldn't bear the thought of you and Laney off hundreds of miles from home."

Luke closed his eyes for a moment as Laney slapped both hands flat against the table and sprang to her feet all in one motion. "Everyone stop for just a minute." She turned the full force of her glare on Luke. "Have you changed our plans without telling me? Because everyone here seems to think you're headed to Oregon and that I'm heading there with you."

Luke stood and cupped her elbow. "Let's go outside and talk."

She jerked away from him. "I'm not going anywhere with you. You've humiliated me in front of the whole family — plus one — now you can just tell me the truth in front of everyone, you low-down, low-down —"

Realizing she wasn't going to come up with an appropriate follow-up, Luke interrupted. "I wasn't keeping anything from you. I just hadn't gotten around to telling you yet."

The hostility in Laney's expression gave way to a worried frown. Luke wanted to hold her close and kiss away that fear; but with the family watching, all he could do was be honest and say what she apparently had already figured out.

"Pa hired Floyd Henderson to run the ranch. He suggested I might want to hitch up with the wagon train in Council Grove in a couple of months. I — I wanted to discuss it with you."

Cold brown eyes stared back at him from a now-expressionless face. "Jane, honey," Laney said without breaking their gaze. "We're leaving now."

"But I didn't get my licorice stick!"

"I'll get you one tomorrow from Tucker's. Get your things now."

The little girl moved to do as she was told. Laney's voice lowered in volume and tone. "Hitch yourself to that wagon train, Luke. But you're not hitching yourself to me, too. And don't think you're going to come back and claim me after you've been gone awhile. No matter how much I ache for you, I'll never leave this town."

"Laney . . ."

She shook her head vigorously, her eyes wide, nostrils flared. "I told you before that Harper is my home. It's my sister's home now, too — look at how attached she already is to your family — and it's even my pa's home until he passes on. This is where my life is. I want to spend the rest of my days here. Get that through your head. I am *never* leaving."

Luke reached for her. "I'll stay. We'll get married like we planned."

Evading his grasp, she moved behind her chair. She spoke as though she had forgotten everyone seated around the table. "I never wanted to be your second choice."

"Second choice?" Did she think he loved Miss DuPres? "Laney, there's no one else."

A short laugh spurted from her lips. "There may or may not be another woman laying claim to your affections, Luke, but that's not even the point. I don't want to be second choice to your lost dream. You'd always blame me that you didn't have a chance to build your own dynasty in Oregon."

"That's not true, honey. Let's just forget about Oregon. I don't want to lose you."

Laney continued as though she hadn't heard him. "You would always be thinking of the what-ifs; and I and any young'uns we had would always be responsibilities rather than gifts from God. If I ever marry, I want to be my husband's first dream, after God — not something he settles for because of a promise. Good-bye, Luke. I don't hold any grudges against you, and I truly hope Oregon is everything you want it to be."

Laney grabbed Jane around the shoulders, and the two left quietly through the door.

Luke watched her leave, pain knifing through him in a way he'd never thought possible.

Silence reigned around the table. Even the children refrained from making comments.

"Oh my," Miss DuPres finally said. "I am mortified at my stupidity. Luke, I beg your pardon for speaking when I had no right."

She sounded so contrite, her face ashen, that Luke softened toward her immediately. He smiled. "It's not your fault, ma'am. I should have brought it up before Laney and I came inside."

Luke pushed in his chair and stepped out onto the porch. He sighed heavily and swallowed hard past a lump in his throat. Even if he wanted to stay in Harper, he'd never convince Laney he wasn't doing it out of some sense of guilt or responsibility.

He let out a groan and raked his fingers through his hair. How had he made such a mess of everything? He had always dreamed of going west, but now he wasn't so sure it was worth it if he had to lose Laney in the process. Suddenly all of his visions of lush green fields gave way to a dismal, brown emptiness of a winter with no snow. What point was there to a dream if he couldn't share it with the one person who mattered?

CHAPTER 14

Idiot, idiot, idiot. The taunt kept up a steady rhythm to Colby's gallop as Laney headed for home. She wouldn't cry. Refused to cry. This was her own fault, and she wouldn't allow herself one tiny bit of self-pity.

The nearer they drew to home, the stronger the dread gnawing her stomach became. She dreaded the smug remarks she was bound to get from Pa when he found out his prophecy about Luke's intentions had come true.

Laney reined in Colby and helped Jane slide from the saddle. "Go inside, sweetheart. I just have to brush Colby down and put him up for the night."

When Laney entered the soddy a few minutes later, Jane was already tucked into bed and snoring softly. Pa was seated at the table sipping a mug of coffee. Surprisingly the dishes he had eaten from were cleaned and put away on the shelf above her rough-hewn counter.

"You must be feeling better," she said grudgingly.

"A mite."

"Good." She cleared her throat. Now what? It was too early to go to bed, and she would rather cut off one of her arms than make polite conversation with Pa while her heart was breaking. She debated going for a walk by the creek, but to do so would be an admission that something out of the ordinary had occurred.

Pa stood. Relieved, Laney walked toward the kitchen. Maybe he would go to sleep so she could be alone with her thoughts. Instead, he grabbed a mug from the shelf, filled it with coffee, and set it down on the table in front of an empty chair. "Sit."

Too startled to rebel, Laney sat. "What's this?" she asked, barely able to keep the sarcasm from her voice. If he was trying to be nice so he could ask for money, he might as well save himself the effort. She'd already given him all she had.

He shrugged his bony shoulders. "Thought you looked like you might like a cup, that's all. Dump it out if you don't want it."

"I didn't say I didn't want it!"

"Well, don't act like I'm about to ask fer

somethin', 'cause I ain't."

Heat rushed to her cheeks.

" 'Sides, I know you done gave everythin' you was savin' just to keep me from goin' to prison. Can't rightly say I know why, but I gotta tell ya, I know what ya gave up."

Laney hadn't mentioned her conversation with Mr. Garner to anyone, let alone Pa. "What are you talking about?"

He regarded her evenly, and for once his face held not the slightest hint of mockery. "Garner stopped by while you was gone."

Laney's hands trembled as they grasped her cup. "So?"

"So he told me to tell ya he'll wait one extra week for the money, but then he has to sell the land and the soddy to his other buyer." Pa gave a snort. "Sounded like he hated to see ya hafta give up yer land."

Realizing there was no sense in pretending, Laney shrugged and sipped her coffee. She set the mug back on the table. "One extra week isn't going to matter much. It would take me six more months to save enough to pay him off like we agreed."

"Where you intendin' on livin'?"

The note of concern in his voice made Laney glance up sharply. She caught his gaze. Was he merely worried about his own hide and where he would sleep, or did he honestly care? Laney steeled herself against the last thought. She would not allow herself to be fooled again. If Luke couldn't love her enough to stay by her side, she couldn't make herself believe someone like her pa was genuinely concerned about her well-being.

"Don't worry," she said, curling her lip in contempt. "I'll figure out something for us. Maybe we could all find a good place to squat — just like old times. Huh, Pa?"

Pa's face darkened. He slapped the table and sprang to his feet. Then he swayed and grabbed on to steady himself. "I ain't stayin' here to be insulted."

"Oh yes you are." Fueled by the humiliation and disappointment of the evening, Laney's temper soared to rage, and she stood to face him. He could hit her if he wanted to. This time she wasn't backing down, and he was going to take what he had coming! "You're going to hear what I have to say if I have to sit on you and hold you down to make you listen! You drank away any pittance we ever had while Ma was alive. Then you made Ben and me live like beggars and thieves until you sold us like slaves to Tarah and Anthony, the only people who thought we had any value." A sob caught in Laney's throat. She paused long enough to acknowledge the prick of conviction, but bitterness had already pushed her too far. Ignoring her conscience, she allowed her tongue to continue on its destructive path. "Do you know what it does to young'uns when their own pa sells them like they're no more important than stock? For years Ben and me worked hard to prove over and over that we aren't like you. Ben made it. He got away. Got a scholarship to seminary and made a better life for himself. I was going to. I tried. But then you had to come back. Now I have nothing — just like you wanted. I hope you're happy, Pa. Because I sacrificed all I had so you could live."

"Why'd ya do it?"

Expecting the back of his hand or a good tongue lashing at the very least, the calm four-word response shocked Laney. "What do you mean?"

"Ya hate me, and I'm going to die anyway. Why give up your land to keep me out of prison? I deserved to go for a lot of reasons, and you know it. It don't make sense."

Laney shrugged. "I don't hate you," she mumbled, knowing full well anything she said to defend her burst of anger would sound ridiculous. "Hating is a sin."

He snorted. "So ya love yer ol' pa, do ya?"

She shook her head, already regretting

that she hadn't listened to her conscience, regretting that she had most likely passed up an opportunity to share the love of Christ with her pa. "To be honest, I don't know how I feel about you. But I do know that God loves you, and He thinks you're worth saving."

"Just like you were worth saving when I sold ya to that teacher and her beau?"

"Just like you were worth saving?" For an instant, Laney felt the impact of his words. An image of the cross flooded her mind.

Tears sprang to her eyes. If Pa didn't deserve her mercy because of the way he had treated her, she didn't deserve God's. Jesus had paid a much higher price for her than she had paid for Pa's freedom. Remorse instantly flooded her. "I'm sorry," she whispered, her heart reaching toward heaven.

"What fer?"

Surprised, Laney caught Pa's gaze. She had been speaking to God, but as she stared into Pa's suspicion-filled eyes, she knew she owed him an apology, as well.

"I've treated you like you didn't deserve love or forgiveness. No wonder you didn't want to hear about Jesus. I paid the money for you to come home because even though I was mad as a hornet at you, I'm different inside than I used to be. I know I don't act like I care anything about you, but the truth is, I don't want you to die and go to hell, and I knew you stood a better chance of staying alive longer if you came home with me. Even though I wish I wouldn't have had to give up my soddy or my land, I'd do it again for the chance to share Jesus with you before you die."

Heavy silence permeated the air between them as Pa sized her up. Then he cleared his throat and sneered. "That just shows how dumb you are."

Laney blinked in surprise. This was far from the repentant response she had hoped for and even halfway expected.

"You know I ain't never held to no religion. I ain't a-startin' now just 'cause you got religion and gave up yer land fer me. Ya shouldn't have done it. I wouldn't have done if fer you." He left her to stare after him as he shuffled to his pallet, practically threw himself down, and lay with his back to Laney.

Bewildered, Laney turned back to her cup. Her own revelation had been so real and poignant that she couldn't believe her pa could be so unmoved. Nevertheless, she knew something had transpired on the inside of her. If not the feelings of love, then at least the willingness to love. Urgency filled her as she listened to her pa begin to cough. *I'm trying, Jesus. Please give me enough time.*

True to Granny's prediction, the townsfolk filled the school-house to overflowing the night of Vivienne's farewell performance. Luke watched the door, wishing — without much hope — that Laney would make an appearance. He wanted . . . *needed* to see her, to somehow make her believe that he loved her and would willingly give up Oregon for her.

He took a seat at the back just as Miss DuPres glided to the front, her red dress shimmering in the lamplight.

"Thank you so much for coming," she said graciously, and the room erupted in applause.

Spellbound, the audience remained completely still while she poured out a haunting rendition of "Lorena."

During intermission, Luke joined several men outside. He noticed Laney leaning against the hitching post. Luke's boots led him in her direction as though they had a mind of their own.

She glanced up and smiled in greeting.

"Been here long?" he asked.

She nodded. "Watching from the door. Granny was right. Folks were happy to show up for another performance."

"She has a lovely voice. We don't get that sort of entertainment around here."

"You think they do out west?"

"I don't know, Laney. And I don't particularly care about entertainment." Luke captured her hand in his and held tightly before she could jerk away. "I want you to listen to me."

"Let go of me!"

"Not until you hear me out."

"Say your piece, then, and make it quick."

Before he could speak his mind, an unfamiliar man wearing a fancy suit and bowler hat interrupted. "Excuse me. Is Miss DuPres performing here tonight?"

"Who wants to know?" Laney asked. From the suspicion clouding her eyes, Luke knew she was thinking the same thing that ran through his own mind. Was this the same man who had abandoned Vivienne and broken her heart?

"I am her fiancé," he replied.

Laney stepped forward, crowding the man's space until he backed up, bewilderment plastered on his face. "What makes you think she wants to see you? Any man who would run off and break a lady's heart ain't worth his salt, as far as I'm concerned."

Luke squirmed. He had the feeling Laney wasn't just directing her words at the wayward fiancé. He almost felt sorry for the man.

Laney moved a step closer. "You'd better give me a good reason not to call the sheriff right now and have you locked up, or that's just what I'm going to do, mister."

"I have all the money right here except what it took me to get to Chicago and come right back." Randy hung his head. "You're right," he said humbly. "I'm not worth the dirt she walks on, but I'll make it all up to her if she'll only take me back."

"If you love her," Laney said, her tone softening, "why did you steal all her money and leave?"

"I was a fool. A swindler. The plan was to wait until she had raised enough money, then leave. I'm ashamed to say I've done it more than once with other women. But Vivienne is so wonderful and kind, I couldn't help but fall in love with her. My relationship with her during the past months has changed me. I made it all the way back to Chicago, then turned around without leaving the train station."

"Well, it's not my place to make Miss Du-Pres's decision for her." Laney heaved a sigh. "Besides, it sounds as though you've learned your lesson. Come on. Let's go find out if she'll speak with you, but I wouldn't count on it if I were you. If you're a praying man, you might want to say one now, and if you're not, you might want to become one."

Stunned, Luke followed along to see how it all worked out. He had expected Laney to run Randy out of town with the sharp edge of her tongue, not find sympathy for a swindler and a cad — even one who claimed to be a changed man.

The room buzzed with conversation while the audience awaited the second half of Vivienne's performance.

"Luke, over here," Pa called as Luke squeezed down the aisle after Laney and Randy. Luke watched them go, then turned toward his parents. This was the first time Pa had been into town since the accident. Ma glowed next to him. He shook Pa's hand and bent down to kiss Ma's cheek. "How are you enjoying Miss DuPres's performance?"

"It's wonderful," Ma said. "Of course, we've had the privilege of hearing her practice lately. But I must say, being at an actual performance is breathtaking."

"Did I see Laney with a stranger?"

Luke nodded. "That was Miss DuPres's fiancé."

"The thief?" Ma asked, her mouth tightening in disapproval.

"He says he's sorry and came back to beg her forgiveness."

"I hope she makes him grovel before she forgives him!"

"Darling!" Pa said, slipping his arm along the back of her seat. "I'm shocked at you."

She smiled and reached up to pat his face. "No, you aren't."

Pa captured her hand and brought it to his lips.

Luke cleared his throat. In moments such as this, he always felt like an intruder. The sort of love Ma and Pa shared was true and lasting. All-consuming at times. A burst of determination fueled a fire inside of him. He said a hasty good-bye and spun around. He was going to find Laney and make her listen to reason.

The lights dimmed. Luke groaned inwardly. He'd have to find a seat before Vivienne started singing again. He slipped into a vacant space in the third row just as she appeared on stage. Her voice seemed richer as she sang with great emotion. Luke had the feeling she had forgiven the man she loved.

The audience clapped wildly at the end of the evening, until finally Vivienne lifted her hand for silence. "Thank you," she said, her face glowing brighter than the brightest star in the night sky. "I would like to share some wonderful news with you. I'm about to be married."

More clapping. Luke smirked. Randy was wasting no time in proving his sincerity. "How would you all like to be my wedding guests?"

The applause continued as Miss DuPres reached toward the side door, where a slightly bewildered-looking Randy stood. He stepped forward and took her hand while the audience stood to its feet, giving an ovation worthy of a New York opera house.

"Reverend," Randy said, finally finding his voice. "Would you, please?"

Anthony made his way to the front. He faced the audience. "Well," he said. "I don't think I've ever had such a large congregation before. I hope to see you all in church on Sunday and just as enthusiastic over singing hymns to God as you are over Miss DuPres and her wonderful singing tonight."

The room filled with laughter, some nervous, some humorous.

Luke glanced around while the couple

said their vows. Where was Laney, anyway? He finally located her watching from the door. Her gaze was focused on the wedding. In the soft candlelight by the door, Luke could see her face clearly outlined. There were no hard lines to make her appear severe. Her lips curved ever so slightly, and her eyes glistened as though she was fighting back tears. Luke swallowed hard. She was so beautiful, he wished he was a painter, able to capture her image on a canvas. He burned her image into his mind, knowing he'd never see another woman as lovely, no matter how long he searched. Suddenly he wanted to tell her so. Ached to hold her. He would never leave her no matter what; and if it took ten years of working on Pa's ranch to convince her he wasn't going anywhere, then that's what he'd do. Because one thing was for sure . . . he wouldn't give up the woman he loved.

Laney felt Luke's gaze even before she saw him. The crowded room faded away, and she saw only the man she loved. She knew he was experiencing the same feelings. She longed to go to him and nearly did so when his lips moved. *I love you.* After only a moment's hesitation, she shook her head, turned, and slipped out the door.

It warmed her to know he meant it. Luke loved her enough to give up going west in order to marry her. But Laney knew what it was like to lose a dream; and even though she'd reconciled herself to her own disappointment, she couldn't let Luke give up on his dream. She loved him too much.

So she hurried to Colby, knowing if she had to face Luke again tonight, amid the romance of renewed love and a wedding, she wouldn't have the strength to turn him away.

"Miss Jenkins."

Laney inwardly groaned at the sound of Mr. Garner's voice. She turned slowly to face him. "Hello, sir," she said.

"I assume your pa told you I was by the other day?"

"Yes, sir." Ashamed, she glanced at the ground. "I'm afraid, Mr. Garner, that even with an extra week, I won't be able to honor our agreement. We'll be clearing out before too long."

"I'm sorry to hear that, Miss Jenkins. I know this isn't your doing."

Tears pricked Laney's eyes. She glanced away and cleared her throat to compose herself. "Thank you."

"Where will you go?"

"Miss Hastings has room for us at her

boardinghouse." It was the cheapest place in town. Miss Hastings was a nosy, grouchy spinster without a sense of humor. The thought of paying to live in a place she would never own seemed like a waste of money, but Laney knew she couldn't afford to be choosy in her present circumstances.

Mr. Tucker had offered her the use of his back room to work, and she had gratefully accepted. She suspected the idea of Granny working there every day appealed to him and had prompted his generosity to waive any rental fees.

From the corner of her eye, she saw that Luke had finally squeezed his way through the crowded schoolhouse and was making his way toward her.

"I have to go, Mr. Garner. Have a wonderful evening."

She quickly mounted Colby and rode off before Luke had the chance to stop her.

CHAPTER 15

"Laney! He–l–l–lp!"

Fear gripped Laney at Jane's cry of distress. She hurried across the wooden floor of her room at Miss Hastings's boarding-house, flung open the door, and made a mad dash toward the stairs.

She stopped short at the sight of Miss Hastings practically dragging Jane up the stairs. Fear widened the child's eyes. Indignation filled Laney, but she bit back angry words. She knew she was in a precarious position, and if she angered her landlady, they'd be out on their ears with no place to go.

Breathless from her swift climb up the long staircase, Miss Hastings stopped at the landing and grabbed her side with her free hand. After taking a moment to compose herself, she turned her furious gaze upon Laney. Laney gritted her teeth as she glanced down and observed her landlady's bony fingers digging into Jane's small arm. The spinster opened her mouth to speak, but Laney halted her. Regardless of the consequences, she would not allow Jane to be hurt.

"First turn Jane loose, Miss Hastings. Then tell me what my sister did to rile you."

The woman's face reddened in anger, and she turned Jane loose so suddenly, the child had to grapple for the railing to prevent herself from tumbling down the steps.

Silently she counted to ten to keep from giving the old hag a quick shove backward. Laney reached for Jane. Once she held her sister protectively to her side, Laney regarded Miss Hastings evenly. "Now what did Jane do?"

"I caught her stealing from me!"

Alarm clenched Laney's gut. "What do you mean?"

"Ask her. She'll tell you."

Laney cupped Jane's chin and forced the little girl to meet her gaze. "Did you steal something?"

Sudden tears filled Jane's blue eyes. "Yes."

Miss Hastings gave a smug nod as though she'd just solved the mystery of the decade. "There. You see?"

Disappointment washed over Laney. Was Jane going to follow in their pa's footsteps?

"For shame. You'll have to give back whatever you took."

The child looked miserable. "I can't."

"Why not. Did you break it?" Laney inwardly groaned, envisioning an expensive vase she would have to pay for.

Jane shook her head. "I ate it."

Blinking twice, Laney tried to assimilate the child's words, but she could only conjure up an image of Jane trying to eat a vase, and it just didn't make any sense. "What do you mean, you ate it?"

Miss Hastings stomped her daintily booted foot in a not-so-dainty manner. "Oh, for pity's sake, the child stole a roll from the kitchen."

Jane cast soulful eyes upon Laney. "It just smelled and looked so good, and I was hungry. So I took it. But I tried really hard not to."

Relief flooded Laney that it wasn't worse; still, she knew her sister had to understand stealing was wrong, no matter what the object of desire.

She glanced down sternly. "Tell Miss Hastings you're sorry and promise never, ever to take so much as another bite of food that doesn't belong to you."

Jane obeyed instantly.

Miss Hastings gave an ungracious sniff.

"Those were to be served with dinner. Since the child has already eaten her share, she will not be given one this evening. And, Miss Jenkins . . ."

"Yes?"

"Please dress appropriately for dinner. I do not approve of your mannish garb." So saying, she spun on her heel and flounced down the stairs.

Laney released a frustrated breath and ushered Jane into her bedroom. The child hopped up on the bed, swinging her legs along the side. She tucked her chin glumly into her palms. "I don't like Miss Hastings one little bit! I wish I had a fat snake to put in her bed. Or a slug or a mess of worms like the ones Will and me dug up last week."

Laney shuddered at the thought of sliding into bed with a mess of squirmy worms, although she had to admit the thought of Miss Hastings doing that very thing contributed greatly to the mirth rising inside of her. She swallowed down the laughter before it reached her face in the form of even a hint of a smile. Composing herself, she recognized that she was the only guidance Jane had, and it was up to her to teach her sister how to treat others — even those who treated a person unfairly. Plastering on as stern a look as possible, Laney eyed the little girl. "Janey! Do you honestly think Jesus would put a fat snake in someone's bed?"

"No," she mumbled. "But He probably never met Miss Hastings."

"Yes, He has. And He loves her just as much as He loves us, so let's try real hard to say something nice about her."

Jane scrunched her nose and closed her eyes while Laney waited. Finally the little girl shrugged, capturing Laney's gaze. "I can't think of anything nice."

It was quite a challenge for a first try, Laney had to admit. "All right. I'll go first, and then maybe you can think of something." Determined to be a good example, Laney searched for something to say until finally, like a stroke of genius, she found her nice thought. "She keeps a sparkling clean boardinghouse, and Granny always says cleanliness is next to godliness. Okay, your turn."

Jane screwed up her face and thought . . . and thought . . . and thought. Suddenly she brightened and glanced up at Laney with a wide grin.

"You thought of something nice to say?"

"Yep. Miss Hastings makes the best rolls I ever had in my whole life!"

Laughter bubbled up inside of Laney and

flew from her lips. She went to the bed and grabbed her little sister, tickling her until their laughter prompted three sharp taps beneath the floor from Miss Hastings's broom. "I will not tolerate such noise."

For someone who couldn't tolerate noise, she could sure yell loud enough to cure a deaf man.

"Shh," Laney said, her eyes still damp with mirth. She laid back and stared at the water-stained ceiling. "Oh, Janey, I promise I'll get us out of here as soon as possible."

Janey cuddled up next to her and rested her silky head against Laney's shoulder. "I don't care where we live, Laney. Just so long as you and me and Pa are together."

"You don't mind living here? Even with mean Miss Hastings fussing at you all the time?"

Her head moved left and right against Laney's arm

"But what about all the fun you had when we played with the baby chicks at the soddy? And what about all the times we sat on the bank and dipped our toes in the creek?"

"I liked that, but it wasn't as much fun when I had to go play at the creek by myself. I reckon there's lots of fun things we can do even here at Miss Hastings's — as long as she don't hear us. Do you think we could find something quiet to do to-gether?"

"Well, yes. I thought we might ask Emily for a reader so I can get you started on your letters. You can practice them while I'm working. Then we can go over them after supper each night. How does that sound?"

"And maybe Pa can listen to me practice, too. He'll probably get awful lonesome over in that room all by hisself. I sure wish we coulda all been in the same room like we was at the soddy."

Laney tightened her grip on Jane's arm. How could two children be raised by the same man and come away so differently? Laney cared where she lived. She wanted stability. Sameness. Jane wanted love above everything else. Family.

With a gasp, Laney sat up. Awareness flooded her like light pushing through a thick, black cloud.

"Are you mad at me, Laney?"

Laney laughed and grabbed Jane for a tight hug. "Of course not! You're wonderful. How did you know that happiness and security don't come from where you live but who you love?"

Jane's brow furrowed with confusion. "I don't know. Did I do something good?"

"You did something very good, sweetheart." Laney bent and pressed a tender kiss to her sister's forehead.

Luke! Laney would have liked nothing better than to run to him immediately, but the downstairs clock bonged six o'clock, a mere half hour before Miss Hastings ordered they be ready for supper. Laney gladly would have foregone a meal to go to Luke, but Jane needed her nourishment. "We'd best get ready so we aren't late for supper."

Jane shuddered a deep sigh. "Yeah. Miss Hastings might get cross if we're late. What are you going to wear?"

"I have a clean pair of britches in the . . . oh." Inwardly she groaned. Miss Hastings had insisted upon appropriate attire. With a sigh, she opened the wardrobe and yanked out her only skirt. She groaned as a telltale rip filled the room.

Jane gasped. "Laney. You tore it!"

Now what? She knew there was no way Miss Hastings would stand for her showing up in britches. She pulled out the blue gown she had made last year.

Jane's eyes grew wide. "Did you make that?"

"Yep."

"It's so pretty!"

Eyeing the gown objectively, Laney grinned. "It is, sort of, isn't it?"

"You going to put it on?"

"I reckon. Why don't you go over and let Pa know we'll be bringing him a tray in a few minutes. I'll come and get you when I'm dressed."

"Okay." She hopped from the bed and scurried out the door, forgetting to shut it behind her. "Pa! Guess what Laney's going to wear?"

A grin tipped the corners of Laney's lips as she crossed the room and closed the door. Twenty minutes later, she was washed and dressed, thanking the Lord she was small enough that there was no need for her to wear a corset. She'd never have managed one alone. After several futile attempts to pin her hair into something resembling a fashionable style, she gave up and let it flow freely down her back.

With five minutes to spare, she left her room and collected Jane. She held her breath, daring Pa to say something. He did. "Ya look jus' like yer ma." Then he turned his back. Laney blinked in surprise as she turned away toward the stairs. She remembered only one kind thing her pa had ever said about Ma: *She was the pertiest thing I ever saw.* Laney couldn't help but smile. Pa was definitely softening.

■ ■ ■ ■

Luke's heart raced until he thought it might beat from his chest. Rusty's hooves pounded the earth. Only one thought hammered in his mind. *Where is Laney?*

He reined in his horse in front of the ranch, slid from the saddle, and skipped all three steps, landing on the porch. Pa opened the door just as Luke was about to barrel through it.

"Slow down, son. What's happened?" Pa hobbled to the bench beneath the front window and sat.

"Laney's gone. Cleared out, lock, stock, and barrel." Panic welled up inside of him. Why had he allowed his pride to keep him from going to her right after the concert? How long had she been gone? How would he find her? "I just came home to grab some gear. I'm going after her."

"I reckon I knew she was clearing out of the soddy."

Luke blinked and stared incredulously. "You knew?"

"Just found out yesterday."

"And you didn't tell me?" How could Pa have done this to him? "I've lost an entire day I could have been on her trail."

"No need to trail her. I know where she is." Pa patted the bench next to him. "Come and sit."

Reluctantly Luke did as he was told. He wanted to go find Laney. The longer he waited, the farther away she would be — even if Pa knew where she had gone.

"I had a visit from Garner a few weeks back, right after the trial. Seems Laney paid off her pa's debt to keep him out of prison."

"Yes, sir. I was there when she offered."

"It was all she had."

The implication of his words hung in the air. "She lost the soddy?"

Indignation washed over Luke. "How could Garner take her soddy away after all the hard work she's done?"

"Now don't go jumping to conclusions. That's why he came to me for advice. He would have offered to give her the soddy or at least have waited until she could raise the rest of the money. But he knew before he asked she wouldn't do it. She's too stubborn."

"So you just let her lose it?"

"Not exactly." His lips twitched.

"Then why is she gone?"

"I bought it from Garner and planned to offer it back to her, but she moved out early."

"You said you know where she went?"

"Took two rooms at Hastings's boarding-house."

Luke's throat tightened. Laney would go crazy closed up in a musty old boarding-house. And what about little Jane? A young'un needed a place to run and play.

Pa reached into his pocket and pulled out a document. He handed it to Luke.

"What's this?"

"The deed to Laney's land and the soddy. I talked it over with your ma. This is our wedding gift to you and Laney."

"I can't take that from you, Pa."

"You ran this ranch while I was laid up. You were even willing to give up the idea of your own ranch to honor your ma and me. We want you to have that land to start your own ranch, just like you've dreamed."

"But Laney won't marry me, and I don't want it without her."

"She will when she sees you're serious about not going to Oregon."

A slow grin found its way to Luke's lips. He headed for Rusty. "Tell Ma I won't be here for supper."

Pa chuckled. "I thought you might not."

Trying to formulate the right words to make Laney listen this time, Luke took it easy on Rusty during the two-mile ride into town.

When he reached the boardinghouse, he dismounted, tethered Rusty to the hitching post, and strode to the front door. He knocked with purpose and waited until Miss Hastings appeared. "Yes?"

"May I see Miss Jenkins, please?"

She glared at him with contempt. "I am afraid Miss Jenkins has retired for the evening."

Flashing his most winning smile, Luke leaned closer. "Miss Hastings, would it be too much trouble to ask her to unretire for a few minutes? I need to speak with her."

Apparently unmoved by what Luke had been assured was a handsome smile, Miss Hastings squinted behind her spectacles. "Come back tomorrow at a decent hour, and I'm sure she will speak with you then."

"I'll speak with him now, Miss Hastings."

Luke glanced up at the sound of Laney's voice. His eyes widened and his mouth fell slack at the sight of her. Laney was always beautiful, but in a gown of blue silk, she was almost more than any man could take.

"I thought you had retired for the evening, Miss Jenkins."

"I would have, except that you reminded me to remove my pa's tray from his room and clean his dishes before I retire."

The pinch-faced spinster's face turned red. "I'll just take that so you can attend to your guest. Please go into the parlor and leave the door open. I run a respectable place, and I will not have my name sullied."

"Of course, Miss Hastings," Laney replied graciously.

Luke would rather have stepped onto the porch or gone for a walk so they could be completely alone, but for the moment he wouldn't argue. He patted his shirt pocket where he had placed the deed. Now if only he could convince Laney that he truly wanted to marry her and stay in Harper.

CHAPTER 16

Laney bit back a grin at the glare on Luke's face. She knew he resented the lack of privacy, but she couldn't afford Miss Hastings's disapproval right now.

"You look beautiful," Luke said, taking her hand as they walked into the parlor.

Laney ducked her head, unaccustomed to such compliments. "Thank you. Miss Hastings doesn't approve of my 'mannish garb.' " She threw him a cheeky grin.

He leaned in close, his tone conspiratorial. "If she ever wants to catch a man, she'd better not insist you wear dresses like this one too often," he drawled. "You overshadow her by a mile."

She laughed, enjoying the glint of admiration in his green eyes, as well as the easy camaraderie they had fallen into as though they had never disagreed. "Why are you flattering me?"

"I'm not. It's all true."

She sank onto the couch. "Have a seat."

He started to sit next to her, but mindful of Miss Hastings pacing the foyer just outside the room, Laney motioned him to a wing chair across from her.

She gathered courage about her like a shield. "I'm glad you've come, Luke. I — I need to speak with you, too."

"What is it?"

Her eyes misted. She longed to sink into his arms, but Miss Hastings's shadow fell across the doorway, keeping them at a proper distance.

"I — I wanted to tell you that I will go to Oregon with you — if you still want me to."

Wordlessly Luke stared at her for such a length of time that Laney thought maybe he hadn't heard her. Finally she cleared her throat. "If you still want me, that is," she repeated.

"If I . . . ?"

"Well?" A frown furrowed her brow. He could say something. Even if he didn't want her anymore.

"No."

"No? You don't want to marry me?" Laney grimaced as her voice reached a high pitch and cracked. She felt the heat rise to her cheeks and wished she could take it all back. She should have let him tell her what he came to say first. He probably would have spared her the humiliation of this rejection by telling her up front he had changed his mind about her.

"I don't want you to go to Oregon."

Laney leaped to her feet. "Yes, Luke. You've made that perfectly clear. Just say what you came to say and get out of here."

"If you don't simmer down and stop that yelling, Miss Hastings is going to be in here throwing me out in two seconds flat."

As if answering a summons, Miss Hastings appeared in the doorway. "Is he manhandling you, Miss Jenkins? Shall I call in Mr. Witherspoon to escort him out?"

Luke grimaced and glared at Laney. "That won't be necessary, Miss Hastings," he said. "Miss Jenkins offered to come west with me . . . and —"

The poor woman's face was instantly stripped of color. "Miss Jenkins, I am afraid I did not realize you were a woman of questionable morals when I allowed you to move into my establishment. Perhaps your peculiar ways should have raised my suspicions, but being a Christian woman, I hesitate to judge a person without proof."

Mortified, Laney flailed her arms at Luke. "Look what you've gone and done, Luke. Miss Hastings, I promise, this isn't the way it appears. I meant I would marry Luke and *then* move west with him."

"Oh, that is a relief." She nodded but didn't quite smile. "You are getting married, then. When will you be moving out? I am afraid I cannot give you a refund for the month in advance you've paid, but I informed you of that fact when you insisted upon paying ahead of time."

"It doesn't matter, Miss Hastings," Laney said glumly. "Mr. St. John has decided he doesn't want me to marry him after all."

"How unchivalrous! I would have expected more from the son of one of Harper's most distinguished citizens."

Something akin to a growl escaped Luke's throat. "Wait!" He took hold of Laney's hand and led her back to the couch. "Sit down," he commanded. Then he strode to the door and extended his arm in that direction. Miss Hastings turned three shades of red and stepped out of the room.

Laney heard her gasp when he pulled the door firmly shut behind her. "Luke, you're going to get me thrown out of here!"

"You don't want to live here anyway." He sat next to her and took her hands. "Now tell me why you changed your mind about coming to Oregon with me. Is it just because you lost the soddy? Because that's exactly the same bad reasoning as it would have been for me to marry you just because I didn't think I'd ever be able to head west."

"That's not it, and it doesn't really matter since you don't want me anymore, anyway. Don't worry about thinking you have to do the right thing by me. I don't go where I'm not wanted!"

"Yes, I know." Luke chuckled. He cupped her chin. "Tell me. What changed your mind?"

Laney gave a sigh. "Jane."

"I don't understand."

"Oh, Luke. Jane made me realize that if you don't have the ones you love around you, it doesn't really matter if you have the best land in the world or not. I can be happier in Oregon with you than I would be on my land, in my soddy, without you."

He bent forward and pressed his forehead to hers.

Laney closed her eyes, savoring his closeness.

"Laney," he whispered, drawing her closer. His mouth moved over hers and clung until she could hardly breathe. All too soon, his lips left hers. He pressed her head against his shoulder.

She wrapped her arms around his waist, resting in the familiarity of his arms. "I meant it, Luke. I'll be happy anywhere, as long as we're together."

"I feel the same way," he said against her hair. "I'd rather stay here with you than go there without you."

Laney pulled away and stared for a moment, trying to wrap her mind around his words. "Then why did you say you didn't want me to go?"

"Because I've already made up my mind not to go west."

Relief nearly overwhelmed her as she looked into his love-filled eyes. Still, she needed to be positive. "But are you sure, Luke? You've wanted it for so long."

"Something changed inside of me when Pa got hurt. What if I hadn't been here to help? I need to stay close to the family. And as far as my land goes, I can raise my own herd right here. It may never be as prosperous as Pa's, but it'll be mine . . . ours, if you'll have me."

"I will, Luke. But where are we going to live?"

"I want to build our herd right here. On your land."

Laney felt the color drain from her face, and she sent him a blank stare. "Didn't you know? I mean . . . why else would I be living here?"

Luke nodded. "I know what you did for your pa." He moved closer and wrapped her in his arms, pulling her close. "I'm sorry I didn't realize the consequences. I would have made sure you didn't worry about your land for even one minute."

She sighed against his shoulder. "Oh, Luke. I think sometimes we just have to be brought low for God to show us the truth about ourselves. I had to realize that my land wasn't the most important thing. God is. And the chance for my pa to come to know the Lord."

"Has he?"

"No, but I'm not giving up. He's softening." Laney gave a short laugh. "He hates it, but he's definitely changing, in spite of himself. I know it won't be long before he accepts Jesus."

"I'm glad to hear it. We'll keep praying for him." He pulled back and studied her, a twinkle lighting his eyes. "How soon can you be ready to move back out to the soddy?"

Was he being cruel? Or had he simply misunderstood? "What do you mean? It's gone. Garner sold it to another buyer already."

Luke grinned broadly, pulled out a document, and handed it over to Laney.

"A deed?"

"Read it."

Her hands began to tremble as she glanced down and read the name on the deed. "Luke St. John." She threw him an accusing glare. "You bought my land?"

"Stop looking at me like that. Pa bought it. Garner wanted you to keep it, but he knew you wouldn't accept an extension. Pa wanted to give you the opportunity to buy it, but when you moved out before he could offer you a deal, he decided to give it to us as a wedding present instead."

"A wedding present? We can't take this. We have to make him let us pay for it."

Luke placed his hand over hers. "It's a gift, honey. A gift. I'm not going to hurt Ma and Pa by trying to pay for it." He slid to his knee in front of her. "You never answered me. Will you share it with me?"

Her eyes misted. "Oh, Luke. You know I will."

Mesmerized by her tears, Luke cupped her face and brought his lips to hers for a brief, tender kiss.

"When can we get married?"

"Wh–when do you want us to?"

"As soon as possible, before something else goes wrong."

"But where would we live? With Pa and

Jane and me, the soddy's awfully crowded already."

"I can add a room on to the soddy for now, and I can start hauling sandstone from the creek to build a real house as soon as possible. It still might take a couple of years before we can move out of the soddy, though. Is that all right with you?"

Laney flung herself into his arms, nearly knocking him backward. "It's wonderful. If you're sure you can put up with Pa. I — I can keep making dresses for Mr. Tucker, and we can save our money for our herd."

Luke frowned.

"What?" Laney asked. Then understanding dawned. "You don't want me to keep working for Tucker?"

Luke smiled, hugged her, then pulled back again to look into her eyes. "I don't guess it would hurt anything, as long as you promise not to get yourself all worn out like you did last fall."

The corners of her lips tilted upward. "I thought you might fight me on that part of it. I don't *have* to work if you don't want me to."

"There'd be an uproar in town if the womenfolk thought I tried to keep you from making their gowns." He grinned. "I guess since the woman from Proverbs could take care of her family and still buy and sell land, my Laney can sew to help build our herd."

"We'll work together," she said, resting her head against his shoulder. Suddenly she jumped up and reached out for him. "Come on."

"Where?"

"You, sir, have to ask my pa for my hand in marriage."

Luke stood and grinned. "Are you sure you want me to?"

Laney laughed. "It's a risk. He might say no just to get under my skin. Then where would we be?"

"Maybe I'd better not ask, then."

"Come on. And maybe while you're at it, you can let him know he's welcome in our home."

Luke pulled her back and wrapped his arms around her. He pressed his forehead against hers. "You've changed," he said softly.

She nodded. "God changed me, Luke. I'm not sure how it happened, really. But all the fighting and anger, it's just not there anymore."

"So I don't guess I have to worry about you flattening me once a day, then?"

She sent him a cheeky grin. "I'm not making any promises. A girl can only change so fast."

"What about the dress? I kind of like it. Think you might wear it again, even without Miss Hastings around to insist on proper attire?"

"I'll wear a dress to church on Sundays."

"Then I'll look forward to every Sunday for the rest of my life."

"And of course I'll keep a skirt handy to pull over my britches when I go to town."

"Of course, we wouldn't want the town dowagers to talk."

Laney smiled and squeezed his hand. "Oh, Luke. I'm so happy it's all finally working out. Let's go tell Pa and Jane."

Luke pulled her back toward him. Laney caught her breath at the love shining from his eyes. Laney's mind filled with the memory of their first kiss. She smiled.

"What are you thinking?" he asked.

"Just that I'm glad I kissed you last fall, or we might never have decided to get married."

"You kissed me? I kissed you after the harvest dance and then asked you to marry me."

Laney regarded him through narrowed eyes. "Luke St. John, you know good and well that if I hadn't kissed you, you never would have gotten up the gumption to admit you love me in the first place. And that was two weeks before any ol' dance!"

His lips twitched, and Laney felt the heat rush to her cheeks. "Oh, you're teasing. Will I ever learn not to get so riled at you?"

"We have a lifetime for you to figure it out." He pulled her close.

Laney smiled as his mouth closed over hers in a kiss very much like the one that had started it all.

EPILOGUE

"Ma! Look at the wildflowers I picked for Grandpa's grave."

Laney pulled up the last of the weeds from Pa's gravesite and sat back on her heels. "They're lovely, Jenny."

She swiped the sweat from her brow with the back of her hand and smiled at her firstborn child. The four-year-old couldn't remember her grandfather, but her curiosity over the source of her given name of Jenkins had forged a bond between the absent grandpa and herself. She loved to hear the stories of her first year of life, when he was her favorite person on earth. Laney smiled to herself as the memories came rushing back.

It hadn't taken long after the wedding for Pa to soften and give his life to Christ. To everyone's surprise, God had given Pa three extra years before He took him home. Pa had learned to read but never read anything but the Word of God. In those years, God truly proved that love could change the hardest of hearts and humble the proudest of men. Pa had doted on his granddaughter and spent every waking hour trying to make her smile — which wasn't a difficult task, considering the baby had lit up like a prairie fire every time he was near.

Laney had grown to love her pa dearly and in the end had shed many tears of grief. Jane's presence helped ease the hurt, and the girl had quickly found a cherished place in the bosom of Luke and Laney's family, as well as the St. Johns' large extended family.

The Double L ranch thrived under Luke and Laney's management. No one could say Luke hadn't proven himself every bit the rancher his pa was.

Laney felt a hand on her shoulder, pulling her from her musings. She glanced up and smiled at her husband as he stooped beside her. "You feeling all right?"

"Wonderful."

"Think it might be today?"

She rubbed her bulging tummy and grinned. "This one's in no hurry, is he?"

"Stubborn like his ma," Luke replied and planted a kiss on her nose.

They anxiously awaited the birth of their

third child. So far they had two redheaded girls; and though Luke adored his princesses, including Jane, he longed for a couple of princes to join the kingdom and even things out a bit. Laney would just be glad to fit into a pair of britches again. With each pregnancy, she had to put them away and don dresses for the last six months. She glanced at her pudgy fingers. She might have to wait a bit longer this time before she could wear them again. She grinned. At least she had a figure now.

"Time to go in and start supper." She reached for Luke. "Help your wife get off the ground."

He hopped effortlessly to his feet and swept her into his arms. "My pleasure," he murmured against her neck.

A gentle breeze blew across the prairie, carrying the fresh scents of spring. The new grass bowed in reverence, and Laney marveled as she glanced out across the land. "Oh, Luke, just look at what God has blessed us with." The pastures teemed with cattle, from last year's stock to the newborn calves. As far as she could see, the land belonged to them.

"God sure knew that His plans for us were right. Thank God I didn't run off to Oregon."

"No regrets?"

"Not even one, honey. Everything I ever dreamed of is right here in Harper — a beautiful family and prosperous land." He captured her lips for a quick kiss, then he smiled, the expression of love in his eyes taking Laney's breath away. "I wouldn't trade any of this for anything in the world."

Tears sprang to her eyes. How good God was to plant their dreams inside of them and then to make them come true.

ABOUT THE AUTHOR

Tracey V. Bateman lives in Missouri with her husband and their four children. She counts on her relationship with God to bring balance to her busy life. Grateful for God's many blessings, Tracey believes she is living proof that "all things are possible to them that believe," and she happily encourages anyone who will listen to dream big and see where God will take them.

The employees of Thorndike Press hope you have enjoyed this Large Print book. All our Thorndike and Wheeler Large Print titles are designed for easy reading, and all our books are made to last. Other Thorndike Press Large Print books are available at your library, through selected bookstores, or directly from us.

For information about titles, please call:
    (800) 223-1244

or visit our Web site at:
    http://gale.cengage.com/thorndike

To share your comments, please write:
    Publisher
    Thorndike Press
    295 Kennedy Memorial Drive
    Waterville, ME 04901